From the Casefiles of
Shelby Woo

THE CRIME: Theft of a ceremonial magnifying glass given by Abraham Lincoln to Allan Pinkerton, the pre-eminent detective of the nineteenth century and head of Lincoln's Secret Service. Because of its historical significance, the magnifying glass is priceless.

THE QUESTION: The magnifying glass was stolen from the Museum of History during the Mystery Ball, an annual party thrown by the Sherlock Society. The thief has to be a member of the Sherlock Society—but who?

THE SUSPECTS: *Mary Longstreet*—As president of the Sherlock Society, she arranged the event and had the best opportunity to plan the heist. She has also had no luck finding investors for her new mystery magazine and is desperate for money to keep it afloat.
Everett Hood—Rich and eccentric, he was originally going to finance Mary's magazine. Their partnership crumbled when both decided to run for president. A sore loser, he pulled his money out when she won. Perhaps he wants to ruin her reputation.
Professor Lance Pickett—Like Shelby's grandpa, he is a member of the criminology department at the local college. He is an avid collector of historical memorabilia and once wrote a biography of Allan Pinkerton.

COMPLICATIONS: The magnifying glass has to be somewhere in the museum, but the police have found nothing. To top it off, each member of the Sherlock Society considers him- or herself an expert detective!

The Mystery Files of Shelby Woo™

Available from MINSTREL Books

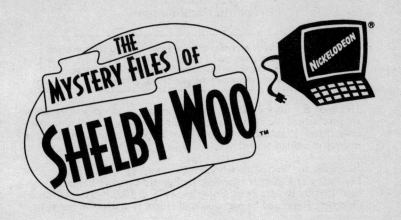

HISTORY MYSTERY

JAMES PONTI

A MINSTREL® BOOK

Published by POCKET BOOKS
New York   London   Toronto   Sydney   Tokyo   Singapore

For Alex and Grayson

"Stopping by Woods on a Snowy Evening" by Robert Frost, from *The Poetry of Robert Frost,* edited by Edward Connery Lathem, copyright 1951 by Robert Frost. Copyright 1928, © 1969 by Henry Holt & Company. Reprinted by permission of Henry Holt and Company, Inc.

A MINSTREL PAPERBACK *Original*

A Minstrel Book published by
POCKET BOOKS, a division of Simon & Schuster Inc.
1230 Avenue of the Americas, New York, NY 10020

ISBN: 0-671-02009-9

First Minstrel Books printing November 1998

10 9 8 7 6 5 4 3 2 1

Cover photography by Jeffery Salter and Tom Hurst

Printed in the U.S.A.

Chapter

1

It's not like my life wasn't challenging enough. I had to balance schoolwork, an internship at the police station, all my chores at my grandpa's bed and breakfast and somehow squeeze in enough time to solve mysteries. Then my grandpa got a great job offer from a college in a suburb of Boston. Faster than you can say, "Don't forget to write," it's good-bye Cocoa Beach, Florida, hello Wilton, Massachusetts.

So now—in addition to my schoolwork, a new internship, and chores—I have to make friends, learn my way around a new city, and get used to the Arctic-caliber snow that seems to be everywhere. About the only kind of mystery I have time to solve now is figuring out what's packed in which box. Which is actually where a real mystery did begin for me last week. I'll open up the case file for you. See if you can help bring the culprit in from the cold.

"It is not a date," Shelby protested as she frantically dug through the pile of shoes she'd dumped onto her bed.

"So you're just acting like a maniac for the fun of it?" replied Angie.

"This is not maniac behavior," Shelby stated as calmly as she could. "I'm just . . . hurrying. There's a significant difference between the two. I want to be ready when he gets here. So we're not late. That's all."

Shelby slipped on one blue shoe and one black shoe to see which went better with her dress. She balanced on one foot like a flamingo looking at the blue shoe in the mirror. Then she hopped on the other and checked out the black. She still couldn't decide.

"It has to be a date," Angie said. "You passed the 'up' test."

Shelby momentarily stopped hurrying and sat

down on the bed. "I'm sure I'll regret this," she said, "but what is the 'up' test?"

"You're dressing up. He's picking you up. You look like you're going to throw up. That's all three *ups*. That means it's a date."

All Shelby could do was laugh. Even though she had just moved to Massachusetts, she already knew that Angie would be the best friend she'd have there. Still, she stayed with her story and claimed that under no circumstance whatsoever was this a date. After all, Vince was "just a friend."

"In that case," Angie said with a sly smile, "wear the blue ones. They don't go with the dress as well, but they'll be more comfortable because the black ones have heels."

The non-date in question was to the Mystery Ball, an annual event held by the Sherlock Society, a local group "dedicated to solving all things mysterious" according to the membership pamphlet on Shelby's desk. Shelby had come across the group's web page and decided to join the day she found out she'd be moving to Massachusetts.

Shelby's grandfather, Mike Woo, came into the room flipping through his brand-new daily planner. She bought it for him to help him get organized. Now it seemed to be surgically attached to his hand. Everywhere he went, he was constantly organizing something.

"Your cousin Cara is coming out for a visit," he said still flipping through the pages. "Do you know the date your spring break starts?" Deep in thought about shoes, Shelby only heard the word *date*.

"It is *not* a date!" Shelby exclaimed much too forcefully. Angie could only laugh as Shelby realized what she'd done. Luckily, Grandpa Mike was too lost in organizing the rest of his life to notice.

Shelby composed herself. "I mean, I'll ask at school this week." Her grandfather nodded and returned to his organizer as he went on down the hall.

Shelby continued to argue her point. "As a member of the Sherlock Society, I automatically received two tickets to the ball. I didn't want to waste one. So I asked Vince to be my—"

"Date," Angie filled in smugly.

"Person driving there in the same car with me," Shelby corrected.

The doorbell rang announcing Vince's arrival.

Shelby hesitated for a moment and quickly put on the black shoes.

"I think the proper term is 'person for whom you wear the prettier, yet slightly less comfortable shoes,'" Angie said.

Shelby ignored the comment and hurried down the stairs. "I got it," she called out to her grandfather. She was determined to beat him to the door. She didn't need him making a big fuss and saying something bound to embarrass her. She already felt awkward enough about the whole thing. Awkward and cold. There wasn't anything she could do about the cold.

The only dressy dress she owned was one she had bought for a summer wedding in Florida. Now she was going to wear it in Massachusetts, in the winter. She was sure she'd freeze to death.

She opened the door to reveal Vince, who appeared to be a little awkward in a coat and tie. They were each taken aback for a moment. Neither had seen the other dressed up before. Vince thought Shelby looked great. Shelby thought Vince looked great. But this not being a date, neither said a thing about it. Instead, Vince just smiled and asked, "Ready to solve a mystery?"

"Absolutely," Shelby replied.

"I'll be back before midnight," Shelby called over her shoulder. She slipped out to the porch and by the time Mike and Angie made it to the front door, Shelby and Vince were already in the car. That confirmed it for Mike.

He turned to Angie and said, "Definitely a date." That was when Angie first realized Shelby's grandfather knew much more about teen life than he let on.

The ball was being held at the Museum of History. Even though it was a short drive, Shelby was glad she wasn't behind the wheel. There was a lot of snow on the road and, despite a few practice sessions with her grandfather, she still wasn't used to driving in it.

Getting used to freezing weather was just one of many adjustments Shelby had to make with the move to Massachusetts. She had to get used to a new school, which meant breaking in a whole new set of teachers. Her weekends were filled helping her grandfather give the new bed and breakfast "that special Woo touch." And, she was still learning her way around the police station where she interned after school.

Hardest of all, she had to get used to the fact that Cindi and Noah weren't around. In Cocoa

Beach the three of them had been inseparable. Now, she only got to "see" them on-line during their frequent internet chat sessions. She missed them so much.

Still she knew she had been lucky to meet Angie and Vince so soon. All three were fast becoming good friends, and Shelby felt comfortable hanging out with them. At least until now. She and Vince were three blocks from the B and B and they'd hardly said a word.

Shelby blamed it on Angie and all her talk about whether or not this was a date. After all, Shelby hung out with Vince all the time and always had plenty to talk about. But now she couldn't come up with a single thing to say.

She thought Vince was a great guy. She couldn't figure out everything that made him tick, but that was part of his attraction. Okay, Shelby admitted to herself, there was some attraction.

"So, what happens at a mystery ball?" Vince asked, finally breaking the ice.

"Pretty simple," Shelby answered. "There's a mystery and there's a ball. The mystery is a contest and the winner will be crowned the Detective of the Year."

"Which I'm sure you'll win," Vince said. "And the ball?"

"Dinner and dancing on the rooftop terrace," Shelby read off the invitation.

"Dinner and dancing?" Vince said. "Looks like those clogging lessons will finally come in handy." They both laughed and Shelby began to relax.

Inside the museum, they followed signs that led them to the third floor. The lobby outside the main exhibit hall was filled with members of the Sherlock Society. Most wore formal wear, although one dressed exactly like Sherlock Holmes, complete with an inverness houndstooth coat and a deerstalker hat. Shelby scanned the room and saw no one else under the age of thirty.

"Definitely a clogging crowd," Vince whispered, looking at two men in tuxedoes. Shelby playfully signaled him to be quiet. She was over her anxiety and was certain it would be a fun night.

At seven twenty-eight, Mary Longstreet, president of the Sherlock Society, was standing in front of the entrance to the exhibit hall with a beefy museum guard as she announced, "In two minutes we will be unlocking this door. Inside is an exhibit called the Art of Detection. It contains over two hundred items related to real and fictional detectives. You'll be locked inside and unable to communicate with the outside world. You'll have exactly two hours to determine which artifact is a fake."

The room began to buzz with anticipation. The guard moved to the door and closely checked his watch. The doorway was flanked by two beautiful arrangements of roses. At exactly seven-thirty, he unlocked the door and all the guests streamed through the entrance. Once the last person was inside, the guard turned the key and locked them in.

Shelby couldn't help but be excited. She had always loved mysteries, but usually worked on them anonymously. Here was an opportunity to show her stuff—in front of a group of adults, no less.

The exhibit was filled with fascinating artifacts. Shelby could have spent an entire day just looking through them all. But there was a two-hour time limit. She'd have to come back another day to check everything out when she wasn't rushed. Tonight she was determined to solve the mystery.

After about an hour and a half, Shelby had narrowed her list down to three possible items: a handwritten letter from Edgar Allan Poe, a magnifying glass given by Abraham Lincoln to Allan Pinkerton, and a police badge issued to Theodore Roosevelt.

She spent the last thirty minutes of the contest closely examining these three items. She tried to look inconspicuous, so none of the other competitors would realize which ones she thought might be fake.

She had studied Edgar Allan Poe in English class and knew that he was one of the first mystery writers. The letter in the exhibit was dated 1844, but the paper was still crisp and white. Shelby couldn't help but think that even her homework didn't look that good. If the letter was over a hundred and fifty years old, it should be yellowing.

Next Shelby checked out the magnifying glass. Allan Pinkerton's name was familiar. Somewhere she had heard of the Pinkerton Detectives, but she couldn't remember where. According to the display card, Pinkerton was a spy during the Civil War and the head of Lincoln's Secret Service. She thought Pinkerton had something to do with trains in the old West, not Abraham Lincoln.

Finally she checked out the badge supposedly worn by Teddy Roosevelt when he was the police commissioner of New York City. Shelby had never heard that Roosevelt had been a police officer, much less commissioner of the nation's largest force. She wished she'd studied harder in American history.

She knew the fake had to be one of these three items.

At nine twenty-five, Mary Longstreet went up to a microphone and announced that there were only five minutes left for people to turn in their ballots. Shelby was frustrated that she couldn't make up her mind. Then she saw Vince, sitting back and watching it all.

She realized that she had practically ignored him the entire night. She had a tendency to get caught up in mysteries and forget the world around her. She went over to him.

"I'm sorry," she said. "I guess I'm not very good company."

"I'm having a great time," he replied. "I've never seen anyone like you."

"What's that mean?" she asked.

"Don't worry," he said. "It's good. So which is it? The letter? The magnifying glass? Or the badge?"

Shelby realized that he'd been watching her and it made her a little self-conscious. She also realized that she hadn't done a very good job of being inconspicuous. She'd have to practice that.

"I think it's the letter," she said. "It just looks too new to be a hundred and fifty years old."

"I should have thought of that," he replied. "Too bad I already turned in my ballot. You better hurry. Time's almost up." Shelby wrote down her answer and dropped it into the ballot box.

Dinner and dancing on the roof-top terrace probably seemed like a great idea back in July when the Mystery Ball was being planned. But, in the middle of winter, it was mostly just a cold idea.

"It looks like an Eskimo prom," Vince said when he saw all the dressed up people clumped around the large outdoor heaters. "So, ready to clog?"

Even though Shelby and Vince joked about the formal nature of the event, they both secretly enjoyed it. Vince even turned out to be a pretty good dancer, despite the fact that he acted like he wasn't. At one point, he gallantly slipped off his jacket and draped it around Shelby's shoulders so she could warm up.

It's a good night, Shelby said to herself.

The band stopped playing and Mary Longstreet went up to the podium carrying the Detective of the Year trophy. For the first time, everybody left the warmth of heaters and moved toward the stage.

"And now, the moment you've all been waiting for," Mary announced as she adjusted the microphone. "As president of the Sherlock Society, it is my pleasure to announce the winner of our contest. Seventy-three people submitted ballots, but only one correctly identified the fake artifact. You may be surprised to learn it was a teenager."

Vince gave Shelby a congratulatory nudge. She smiled broadly and began to think it was a *very* good night.

"So, it is a great honor to introduce the Sherlock Society Detective of the Year," Mary continued, "Vince Rosania."

Shelby and Vince were shocked. He had just filled out a ballot for the fun of it and hadn't put much thought into it. He was so surprised, in fact, that Shelby had to remind him to go up to the podium and get the trophy.

There was a hearty round of applause for Vince as he walked up onto the stage. Shelby was happy for him, but she was also a little jealous—maybe a lot jealous. With all the changes she was going through, one of the few things she had confidence in was her ability to solve mysteries. Now, even that was in question.

Vince gave a typically Vince-like acceptance speech. He just held his trophy and said, "Thanks." That's it. No explanation of how he solved the case. No mention even of which exhibit was, in fact, the fraud.

Mary rushed to the microphone and filled everyone in on what they were dying to find out. It turned out the fake artifact wasn't the letter or the magnifying glass or the badge. It was a medal awarded to a detective and inscribed, "For Brave Service During World War I."

The inscription seemed odd to Vince. After all, it couldn't have been called World War I until there was a World War II. But that solution seemed too simple, which is exactly why nobody else noticed it. They had all been looking for difficult clues and in the process ignored the most obvious one.

Shelby was mad at herself for being jealous.

Vince was a good friend and she should have been nothing but happy for him. She knew she'd have to think hard about this and try to be more mature. But she also knew that would have to wait, because she saw something even more distracting.

Detective Sharon Delancey was standing at the door to the terrace with a handful of police officers. Detective Delancey was Shelby's superior at the police station. But she wasn't supposed to be at the ball because she was on duty. Shelby knew that something was up when the officers started blocking all the exits.

Detective Delancey went up on the stage and whispered to Mary Longstreet. Whatever she said obviously upset Mary very much because Mary quickly left the stage and went over to a police officer who was talking to the museum security guard from earlier. The detective was left alone on the stage.

"Ladies and gentlemen, I regret to inform you that the Mystery Ball is now over," Delancey announced. "Furthermore, one of you is under arrest. And until I figure out which one, no one is going anywhere."

Chapter
2

"How could this happen?" Mary Longstreet cried as she impatiently paced back and forth. "How could someone have stolen Pinkerton's magnifying glass from right beneath our noses?"

Shelby couldn't believe it either. Ninety minutes earlier, she had been examining the magnifying glass. Now it was missing and she didn't have a clue how the crime had been committed. She absentmindedly bit a fingernail and stared off into space.

"What are you thinking?" Vince asked her.

"Well," Shelby replied, "the door to the exhibit hall was locked the entire time we were in here. No one came or went. That means the thief has to be someone in this room."

Vince nodded his agreement. The two of them looked at the faces around them. As hard as it was to imagine, they knew that one of those faces belonged to a thief willing to steal a priceless piece of American history. Detective Delancey knew it too. That's why she and the other police officers decided to question each person before escorting them out of the museum.

Delancey had everyone wait in the cafeteria. It was an ideal spot because it was large, well-heated, and away from the exhibits. She didn't want anyone sneaking around and tampering with evidence.

"We'll do this as quickly as possible," Delancey announced to the assembled group. "Your cooperation in that regard is greatly appreciated. For the sake of organization, we'll hold the interviews alphabetically."

Shelby had been through enough roll calls in her life to know that "alphabetically" meant she was in for a long wait. Which is exactly what Delancey wanted. She needed Shelby in the cafeteria as long as possible.

"No one knows you work at the station," Delancey whispered to her intern. "Keep it that way."

Shelby smiled. She knew what the detective was after. People are extremely cautious when they talk to the police, but they don't pay much attention when they talk in front of a teenager. Shelby was to be Delancey's secret set of ears.

Shelby loved that Delancey let her do more than the filing and odd chores that made up her official duties around the squad room. Sometimes the detective would bounce theories off her. She even let her sit in on a few interviews. But this was the first time Delancey had ever trusted Shelby to do something completely on her own.

Shelby was thrilled but also troubled because she didn't know how to do it. She couldn't just wander around the cafeteria eavesdropping on everybody. She had to figure out a way to get them to come to her.

"That's a crucial bit of information," Vince said.

"A clue?" asked Shelby.

"No, free hot chocolate." He motioned to a hot

chocolate machine in the middle of the cafeteria. That solved Shelby's problem.

"Perfect," Shelby said with a smile. "Let's sit by it."

"I don't think sitting by it will warm you up much," Vince countered. "You probably need to drink it."

"And on a night like this," she explained as they walked across the room, "so will everybody else. It's the perfect place to listen."

Shelby planted herself in a booth right next to the machine while Vince went to get their first cups.

"I talked to one of the police officers," he told her. "They're letting me go with the W's, so I don't have to leave before you." He squirted a dollop of whipped cream on top of the cocoa and handed it to Shelby. "You better keep warm." Shelby smiled and hugged Vince's jacket a little tighter.

Figuring out who committed a crime is easy compared to figuring out what some guy is thinking. Boys are the real mystery to me. Vince is a classic example. I have no clue what he feels about anything.

A week after meeting Angie, I knew everything about her. I mean everything, from her favorite rock groups to her deepest secrets. I'd known Vince for over a month before he even mentioned he had a little sister. And he worships her. You think she would've come up before that.

He's so hard to read that when I first met him, I thought he was a suspect in a series of crimes that had been committed in the school auto shop. Now I'm with him at the Mystery Ball. And I still have no idea what he thinks about school. About mysteries. Or about me.

"So, who do you think did it?" Vince asked.

"You're the Detective of the Year," teased Shelby. "You tell me."

Vince just rolled his eyes and laughed. "Let's see." He pretended to be deep in thought. "It wasn't me."

Shelby played along. "It wasn't me."

"That's two down," Vince reasoned. "See, this detective stuff isn't so hard."

While Shelby and Vince waited for people to pass by their table, Detective Delancey and three other officers conducted interviews down the hall in the Constitution Room.

The room housed an exhibit on members of the Continental Congress that were from Massachusetts. Because Delancey was the ranking officer, the others playfully insisted she should sit at the replica of John Hancock's desk. (He had been president of the Congress.) They then began to refer to her as "Madame President." (She kind of liked it.)

Despite the good humor of her co-workers, Detective Delancey was not in the best of moods. She had been ready to go home and get some much needed sleep when the museum guard called to report the burglary. She knew the interviews would take a while—a long while. Not only were there a lot of people to question, but each person thought of him or herself as the reincarnated Sherlock Holmes.

Delancey had to listen to an endless series of unsolicited theories during the course of her interviews. Each one seemed more ridiculous than the preceding one.

"It was all done with microscopic lasers and tiny mirrors," suggested one woman.

"I don't believe the magnifying glass was ever

really there," claimed another. "We were all just hypnotized into thinking we saw it."

Delancey's favorite was the man in the houndstooth inverness coat. He showed her his driver's license to prove that not only did he dress like Sherlock Holmes, but he also had his name legally changed from Melvin Jenkins to Sherlock Holmes.

"Someone told me they saw a suspicious man with five trained cockroaches," he whispered conspiratorially. "Very well trained."

Delancey decided to play along for the fun of it. "And you think the cockroaches carried out the actual heist?"

"Elementary, when you think about it," he replied.

"Who told you about the roaches?" she asked in hushed tones.

"Dr. Watson, over there." He nodded toward a ventriloquist's dummy he had dressed like Holmes's literary sidekick.

"I'll question him later," Delancey reassured him.

Despite the crackpots, Delancey was getting a pretty consistent review of the night's events. Everyone reported seeing the magnifying glass until nine-thirty, when they were led out of the room to the terrace. The security guard called the police station at precisely nine forty-three. That left only thirteen minutes during which the robbery could have occurred.

Several people reported that a man named Lance Pickett had refused to go out on the terrace for dancing. While everyone else was outside, he sat alone in the hallway reading. Delancey decided to break the alphabetical mode and called him in.

Pickett was a tall man with a goatee. All through the interview, he coughed into a handkerchief.

"Why didn't you go out onto the terrace with everybody else?" Delancey asked him.

"It was too cold out there," he answered. "I'm just getting over the flu and can't afford to get sick again." He reached into his coat pocket and pulled out the medicine he'd been taking.

"So you were just going to sit inside the hall for the rest of the night?" She wasn't buying it and it was making him nervous. He nervously rapped a distinctive silver ring against the tabletop.

"No. I was just reading these brochures and waiting to find out who had won the contest," he explained. "I wanted to know which artifact was fake." He had a handful of brochures that had been left on a table by various society members advertising businesses and services.

Meanwhile, Shelby continued to maintain her post by the hot chocolate. She was right. Most everyone did come by. Unfortunately, they all seemed just as confused as she was about the theft.

She did overhear part of one heated discussion, though. "Look over there," she said to Vince. Mary Longstreet got into an argument with an older, aristocratic-looking man.

"I blame all of this on you," he barked at her. "This event was poorly conceived from beginning to end. It will destroy the reputation of this organization." To emphasize his point, he rapped the floor with the silver tip of his cane. Shelby got the impression the cane was just for show because he didn't really use it to help him walk.

A red-faced Mary stalked off and the two remained separated on opposite sides of the cafeteria. Fifteen minutes later Shelby learned his name was Everett Hood when an officer came in and called him for his interview.

Shelby wrote the name on a napkin.

"You know, Mary Longstreet might be the one," Vince suggested. "While we were all on the terrace, she was sorting through the ballots. She would have had plenty of time to swipe that magnifying glass."

Shelby couldn't believe it. First he wins the contest, she thought. Now he's coming up with a prime suspect. A prime suspect I should have thought of.

"It's worth considering," she told Vince.

"Think about it," he continued. "She prepared this whole event. It was a surprise to everybody else. She was the only one who had ample opportunity to plan the robbery."

Shelby was devastated. Vince was solving the case right in front of her. More important, he was solving the case without any help from her. Shelby noticed the clock on the wall. It was almost midnight. She was going to miss her curfew.

"I gotta find a phone and call my grandpa," she said.

"Over there." Vince pointed to a pay phone on the wall. He dug into his pocket and pulled out a quarter.

"Why don't you stay here and keep your ears open," she suggested.

"Sure thing," he responded. "I'll try not to solve it without you."

Shelby laughed, but secretly that's exactly what she worried would happen. She hurried over to the phone and called her grandfather. She told him everything that had occurred and the state of the investigation and then assured him she'd be home as soon as possible.

When she was done, she went back to the booth and continued to listen for clues as the room emptied one person at a time. Shelby and Vince were the last to be called in to be interviewed.

Delancey was frustrated. Most everyone had a pretty solid alibi. Furthermore, they had searched every briefcase, bag, and pocketbook. They had looked everywhere and there was no sign of the magnifying glass.

"No one left during the event, right?" she questioned the two.

"Not a soul," replied Shelby.

"It's still got to be in the exhibit hall," Delancey announced to the other officers. "Start at the terrace and search every inch of it." She

rubbed her temples to fight back the ever growing headache.

Shelby and Vince went over everything they
saw and heard that night. Shelby told Delancey
about the argument between Mary Longstreet
and Everett Hood. Delancey added that a few
people mentioned seeing them arguing earlier
when everyone was going to the terrace. Shelby
told her Vince's theory about Mary Longstreet,
making sure to give him full credit.

"Very impressive," exclaimed Delancey. "First
he wins Detective of the Year, then he comes up
with best theory of the evening."

Vince smiled sheepishly.

"Looks like someone might give you a run for
your money," she said to Shelby with a wink.

They talked for about thirty minutes before
Delancey told them to go home and get some
sleep. It was after two when Vince and Shelby
finally walked out of the museum and got into
his car. They were both exhausted, and Shelby
closed her eyes and rested her head against the
passenger-side window.

Vince turned the key and started the ignition
and the defroster. Neither of them noticed the

car on the other side of the parking lot follow them onto the street.

Shelby couldn't believe how late it was. She had to get up early the next morning to help her grandfather. She was certain he'd have a long list of things to do in that organizer of his.

Vince fumbled with the radio looking for a station with mellow music. He didn't pay attention to the other car until he had made three turns. Then he noticed it was still behind him. He began to wonder if it was following them. At a stop sign, Vince acted as if his engine were cutting out.

"What's the matter?" Shelby asked, opening her eyes.

"I'm just not sure about that car behind us," Vince answered.

He continued to act as if his engine were stalling out. He waved for the other car to pass. After a few moments it pulled around him. It was really dark and there weren't a lot of streetlights. Vince could only tell that it was a dark blue or black Jeep. And there was no way he could make out the licence plate number. The windows were tinted and he couldn't even see the driver.

"What aren't you sure about?" Shelby asked.

"It was stupid," he answered. "I thought that car was following us."

"You've got mysteries on the brain," Shelby reasoned. "Don't worry. I know the feeling well."

Three blocks later, they noticed the car again. This time Shelby didn't think it was Vince's imagination.

"This is not good," she said. Her knees started bouncing with nervous energy.

"Someone must have seen us talking with Detective Delancey or something," he answered. "Let's see if we can lose him."

Vince accelerated and the other car stayed right with him. A light snow had fallen, which made the roads slippery. When Vince made a sudden turn the back of his car fishtailed.

Shelby tried to figure out where they were, but she was lost. She still didn't know her way around town very well, certainly not late at night and going this fast. She tried to get a glimpse of the driver, but she was blinded by his headlights. Then she had an idea.

"Are we near the police station," she blurted out. "We could pull into their garage."

"Perfect." Vince changed gears. "He can't follow us in there." He made a quick turn and headed for the police station. The other car stayed right on their tail. Despite the temperature, Vince was feeling hot. He had to wipe the sweat out of his eyes. He didn't see the patch of ice on the road ahead until it was too late.

When his headlights reflected off the ice, he tried to slam on his brakes, but there was no stopping the car. It skidded across the ice and slid out of control. Before Shelby knew it, they were sliding sideways off the road and heading straight for a concrete wall surrounding an enormous house.

Chapter
3

A million things raced through Shelby's mind as the car slid off the icy road. Mostly, she felt utterly out of control. She was at the whims of force, acceleration, inertia, and all those other scientific laws of motion. She didn't care for them when she had to study them for a test. She certainly wasn't fond of them tossing her around like a human science project.

Vince tried to regain what little control was possible. The view through the windshield was a lot like a virtual reality race-car game he loved to play at the arcade. Except there he knew he could always walk away from the spectacular crashes.

Even though his instincts made him want to hold his foot down on the brake, he knew that made his car little more than a sliding slab of steel. He had to force himself to pump the gas in an attempt to get the wheels to pull out of the slide and away from that concrete wall.

The back wheels spun wildly, spraying chunks of ice onto the sidewalk. Finally they dug into the asphalt and sent the car lurching in another direction. It came to a jarring halt, missing the wall by only two feet. They were safe, but only momentarily. They looked up to see the other driver barreling right toward them.

Shelby shielded her eyes from the headlights. At the last second the other driver veered around the ice patch and disappeared down the darkened street. Vince let out a huge sigh of relief. He looked over at Shelby, her eyes shut tight.

"You can look now," he ventured.

Vince reached over and tapped her on the shoulder. Shelby tried to catch her breath, but her heart was racing too fast.

"I don't suppose there was some insanely jealous boyfriend down in Florida you forgot to warn me about," he wondered. "One that was extremely jealous and known for his unsafe driving habits?"

"No." Shelby smiled between quick breaths. "No boyfriend."

"That's good," he said. "Of course that must mean someone was after us because of tonight. So, you going to be okay?"

"Yes." She took in another deep breath. "I'm just a little spooked."

"I don't know how it happened," he said obviously upset. "I'm so sorry."

"No. You were great," replied Shelby. "It was dark. There was no way to see that ice. I don't know how we missed that wall. But you were great."

They were quiet the rest of the way back to the bed and breakfast. Vince drove slowly and made sure to keep a lookout for the other car. There was no sign of it. Finally they pulled up to the house and Vince walked Shelby to the door.

"Well, you made it back in one piece," he offered.

"That's got to count for something," she replied.

He flashed a broad smile that masked his total sense of confusion. Vince had been dreading this moment ever since Shelby had invited him. He didn't know how to say good-bye. Should he kiss her? Should he hug her? He had planned to make a judgment call based on signals he got during the evening. But that was before he knew it would be an evening filled with high crime and life-threatening escapes. There wasn't a lot of time for signals.

He didn't see a clean shot to kiss her, so he ruled that out. After all, she was a good friend and a mistimed kiss could ruin that friendship. Likewise, a hug didn't seem quite right. It seemed especially anticlimactic considering the car chase. So, he opted for the lamest cop-out he could come up with.

"I had a great time," he said.

Then he shook her hand.

Shelby almost laughed out loud. What is he, she thought, a banker? She didn't know what to make of the gesture, but sure felt silly shaking her friend's hand.

"Me too," she responded. After another awkward moment Vince started back to his car.

It never dawned on Shelby that Vince might be just as confused about all this as she was. Then she heard it. Heard him speaking out loud—it was faint because he was walking away. But she heard him all the same: "Robberies, car chases, and ballroom dancing? I can't imagine what'll happen on the second date."

"Angie was right," Shelby whispered to herself. "It was a date."

Shelby couldn't believe herself. On a night when she was in a car spinning wildly out of control—a night when she was practically an eyewitness to the theft of a priceless museum artifact—her most pressing thoughts were about a handshake and what technically was or wasn't a date.

I'm such a goober, she thought as she put her head on her pillow. The excitement of the night's events quickly gave way to Shelby's desperate need for sleep. She knew her alarm would buzz soon enough and she could try to figure everything out then.

Shelby was dog tired when she joined her grandfather for their new Saturday ritual—unpacking. They had fought the battle of the boxes every Saturday since they'd moved to Massachusetts and there was no end in sight.

She ripped open a box and something caught

her eye. It was a bumper sticker for C.J.'s, the hamburger joint she used to hang out at with Cindi and Noah. She still had trouble believing she'd moved away from them. It had all happened so quickly.

They'd considered the move the previous summer when Grayson College offered Mike Woo a position teaching in their criminology department. It was a great opportunity, but he wasn't sold on the idea until he saw a bed and breakfast for sale in the area. It needed some fixing up, but he knew it would be perfect. With the extra income, he could save enough money to send Shelby to college.

Shelby reluctantly agreed. She hated leaving Cocoa Beach, but part of her was excited about the adventure of moving to a new city. It had been hard for her to adjust to the change from China to Cocoa Beach, but, in the end it had been worth it. She hoped this change would also turn out for the best.

It wasn't going to be easy. It would take time, and adjustments would have to be made. The day she arrived in Massachusetts, she sat down to make a list of all the things she didn't like about the situation. She filled three pages. Front and back.

Each night she'd look to see if there were any items she could cross off. After a few months the list had dwindled down to two items. The first was "No Cindi and Noah." She'd never be able to cross that one off. The second was "Too much work to do at the inn." It didn't seem like she'd ever be able to cross that one off either.

She liked the new bed and breakfast. She even liked it better than the one in Cocoa Beach. It was older and had a lot of character. That's what had sold Mike on its promise. There was a room that had once been a chapel. Inside it were high, crescent windows that caught all of the light during the sunset. It was a great thinking spot. (That's where she sat the night she made her three-page list.)

Her favorite room, though, was the library with floor-to-ceiling bookshelves on every wall. She liked everything about the room. It even had a great wooden smell to it. It had taken three Saturdays of unpacking to get all the books arranged, but now the room was perfect.

Angie dropped by around noon. She was a fairly regular participant in Saturday unpackings. (Shelby thought she must be a glutton for punishment.) In truth, Angie really liked Shelby and liked hanging out with her. Shelby felt the same.

Shelby thought Angie was the most focused person she had ever met. She had two great passions. Angie was a marvelous science student, having twice won the school science fair. Shelby had no doubt that she would one day become a top-flight scientist. She was also a die-hard Boston Red Sox fan. Each year, on the day after the Red Sox were eliminated from championship contention, Angie wore all black to school. Shelby had no doubt that one day Angie would throw her good luck baseball right through the television screen when the Sox blew yet another late inning lead.

"Tell me about last night," Angie said with an expectant don't-hold-anything-back look.

"Long story," replied Shelby.

"My shift doesn't start at the video store until five-thirty." Angie worked part-time at the neighborhood video store. "Where are we unpacking today?"

"Library, again," replied Shelby.

The two of them sat down on the floor of the

library and started digging through boxes for items Mike needed taken to his office at school.

"So, was it a date or not?" Angie was nothing if not direct.

"I don't know," Shelby declared honestly. "It's so hard to tell, what with the robbery and the car chase."

Angie stopped cold. "When you say long story, you mean it. Details, please."

Shelby went on to tell Angie everything about the Mystery Ball. Everything except the part about being jealous of Vince. And the part about Vince's referring to it as a date. She knew she couldn't live that one down. But she did tell her everything about the stolen magnifying glass.

"It's not just the theft that's baffling," Shelby explained. "It's the fact the thief was able to get the magnifying glass out of the museum. All of us were together. All of us got searched. I can't figure out how someone could do that." Shelby mulled it over for a moment.

"I got it," Mike shouted from across the room. Shelby spun excitedly.

"You figured it out?" Shelby asked.

"No, I got my favorite cookbook. I've been looking for this since we moved here." Mike took the book out of the box. "I'm going to make you two a great lunch." He hurried out of the room for the kitchen.

"So, who are your suspects?" asked Angie.

"It's hard to say," Shelby admitted. "There's Mary Longstreet. She's the president of the Sherlock Society. She had the best chance to do it, but I don't know any motive she might have.

"There's a rich guy named Everett Hood, who started an argument with Mary—even before the robbery. I don't know what they were fighting about. But he certainly didn't play well with others."

"Robberies, arguments—this is a pretty rough crowd," teased Angie.

"There was also some stranger named Lance Pickett. He's the only person who didn't go out onto the terrace. I think he's Detective Delancey's prime suspect."

Shelby thought about the three suspects for a moment. "Beyond that," she continued, "I don't know of any."

They went back to the boxes. "Look at this!" Angie cried. From the box she pulled a faded photograph. It was Mike Woo's graduation picture from the San Francisco Police Academy. In the picture, Shelby's grandfather was young and intense with a military crew cut.

Shelby marveled at it.

Just then Mike came to the door. "Time for lunch," he announced. The two girls stared for a moment and then burst out laughing.

"What?" he asked. They looked at him and looked down at the picture.

"You were so cute," they said in unison. Shelby held up the picture for Mike to see.

"That was some other guy posing as me," Mike tried to cover. "I was never that young."

They went to the kitchen table, where Mike served them a vegetable-and-rice dish that he had christened Woo's Five-Minute Miracle. It more than lived up to its name.

"You've outdone yourself, Mr. Woo," Angie said.

"Now you know why I've been looking so hard for this cookbook," he explained. "It's got all my specialties." He turned to Shelby. "How was the exhibit at the museum?"

"It was great. We've got to go back together," Shelby said. "Do you know anything about Allan Pinkerton?"

Mike ticked off Pinkerton's history: "Nineteenth-century detective. Founded the Pinkerton National Detective Agency, which worked mostly on railroads. He stopped the first assassination attempt against Abraham Lincoln."

Shelby and Angie were stunned.

"What?" he kidded. "You think I'm just a cute guy with a crew cut? I teach this stuff, you know."

"I just didn't realize you were an expert on him," pleaded Shelby.

"He's an important figure in the history of criminology," Mike continued. "But I'm no expert. But there is a professor down at the college you should talk to. He's an expert. He even wrote a book about Pinkerton."

"Really." Shelby was excited. "Do you have a copy?"

"Sure," Mike said. "Somewhere in the library." He headed out the door and Angie turned to Shelby.

"Considering how long it took him to find the cookbook," Angie said, "you might want to take a look at your local library instead."

Mike, however, was back in just a few moments. He had the biography in his hand and dropped it in front of Shelby.

"Here you go," he said.

The title was *Allan Pinkerton: The Relentless Search For Justice.* Shelby flipped it over and saw the picture of the author on the back cover. She recognized the face instantly.

The author was Lance Pickett.

Chapter
4

Shelby couldn't believe her eyes. Lance Pickett was staring at her from the back of the book. She read the brief description of the author beneath his picture. It claimed he was one of the foremost scholars on the life and times of Allan Pinkerton.

"Grandpa," Shelby said as she considered the new information, "Angie and I were thinking of driving those boxes over to the college and unloading them for you."

Angie stopped midway through a bite of Woo's Five-Minute Miracle. "We were?" This announcement was news to her. Shelby's brutal stare told her something was up.

"I mean, yeah," Angie played along. "We were just about to call Vince and get him to help us." Another Shelby stare. Angie had no idea what was up.

"Actually, we were going to leave Vince out of it," Shelby informed Mike and Angie in the process. "We're quite capable of moving a few boxes ourselves."

"Right, right," a confused Angie responded before giving up. "Whatever she just said." She went back to the rice.

Mike was only too happy to let the girls move the boxes. He had a few guests and not much time to run over to the college. He slipped Shelby some money so the two of them could go out for hamburgers afterward.

On the ride over to the college, Shelby tried to explain the significance of what she had just learned. "Don't you see?" she exclaimed. "Lance Pickett is the one person with a weak alibi. And now he turns out to specialize in the life and times of Allen Pinkerton. That would make him a prime suspect in the theft of a Pinkerton artifact, even if he had a good alibi."

"That part, I understand," claimed Angie. "I'm just stumped at the part where you didn't want Vince to help us move all those heavy boxes."

"We're modern women," Shelby protested. "We don't need some guy around just 'cause there's a little manual labor."

"Aren't you the girl who keeps conning him into shoveling the snow off your walkway?" Angie reminded her. Shelby ignored the comment.

Angie pulled her car onto the picturesque campus of Grayson College. The redbrick liberal-arts school had quite a few excellent departments, most notably it's highly regarded department of criminology. Shelby was considering going there after high school. Her tuition would be free because her grandfather taught at the school.

But that Saturday afternoon Shelby and Angie weren't thinking about the school's history—and they weren't admiring its architectural beauty. They were bemoaning the fact that the criminology department was located on the fourth floor of the building.

"I think being a modern woman is highly overrated," a red-faced Angie said as they heaved the final box of textbooks up the last few steps.

Shelby searched the ring of keys Mike had given her and unlocked the suite of offices that made up the department. Despite the staid academic setting there were touches of police humor throughout. A sign next to the student phone guaranteed "All prisoners have the right to one and only one phone call." And the area where I.D. photos were taken was made to look exactly like the mug shot set-up at a police station.

"Helloooo," Shelby called out, her voice echoing through the room. "Anybody here?" There was no response. "Good," Shelby said as she started sliding boxes of books across the slick tile floor.

"Why is that good?" Angie followed behind with another box.

"If we're alone we can check out Professor Pickett," Shelby explained. "I wonder which office is his." She scanned the row of office doors that made up what the professors called The Cell Block. There were no nameplates, so she couldn't figure out which office belonged to Pickett.

"Disgusting," Angie said as she entered

Mike's workroom. "Is this an office or a shrine?" Indeed the room had quite a few pictures of Shelby.

"He's sentimental," Shelby offered in defense. She sat down at her grandfather's desk and began searching through his papers.

"What are you looking for?" asked Angie.

"A list of what professor uses what room," said Shelby. "I need to find Pickett's office to look for clues." Something caught her eye and she picked up a sheet of paper. "This'll do. It's a list of office phone extensions."

"No one's here," reminded Angie. "Who are we going to call and ask?"

"Pickett," replied Shelby. She picked up Mike's phone and dialed Pickett's extension. Seconds later, they heard a ringing farther down the cell block. "I think that's for us," she teased.

Angie shook her head. "Of course," she thought. All they had to do was follow the ringing.

Once they found the office, Shelby started searching through Mike's master keys, looking for one that would unlock Pickett's door. She tried seven keys before—presto—the door opened.

The office was immaculate; not a thing was out of place. Books were arranged along the shelves by size. Photographs were neatly arranged and facing the same direction. One wall held only diplomas. Another wall held only awards he had received from various book and history groups for his biography of Pinkerton.

"I hate neat people," Shelby snarled. "They never leave good clues."

The two of them started to look for anything that might be telling.

"He's been here today," said Angie.

"What?" Shelby wondered. "You read minds now?"

"No. Newspapers." Angie pointed to a perfectly arranged stack of used newspapers in a recycling bin. Sure enough, the top paper was from that morning. The front page article on the theft had been cut out.

"You're getting good at this," complimented Shelby. Angie smiled and resumed looking. She really enjoyed this detective stuff.

Shelby saw that Pickett had written a phone number on that day's calendar page. She jotted the number down on a slip of paper. Then a look of panic washed over her face.

"What?" asked Angie.

"That," said Shelby, pointing at a jacket hanging on the back of the door. "What are the odds he went home without his jacket?"

Angie realized that Pickett could walk in at any moment. Suddenly she wasn't enjoying this detective stuff all that much after all.

They instantly left the office, careful not to disturb a thing. The potential close call made Angie a little jumpy. "Can we go now?" she asked once they were back in Mike Woo's office.

"Just a minute. We still have to put a box in the evidence room," said Shelby.

"What's the evidence room?"

Shelby picked up the final box and started to carry it to the end of the hall. "You're gonna love it."

At the end of the hall of offices, there was a cage door that led to a maze of cabinets and shelves. It looked a lot like a police station's evidence room, and was in reality a storage area. It's where the professors stored anything too bulky or valuable to keep in their offices.

Even though the caged front let in air, the room reeked of a collection of indistinguishable smells. Everything was dark and dusty.

"Police work seems pretty creepy," Angie observed as she scanned the shelves of antique equipment like early fingerprint kits.

"Be careful," warned Shelby. "It's easy to get lost back here."

"Time to leave." Angie had turned to face a shelf filled with human skulls. "Definitely time to leave."

"Come on, Angie," Shelby said. "You're a woman of science. Sometimes the police have to find clues in dead bodies. It's called forensic evidence."

"It's called Creepsville," Angie shot back. "Besides, I've always specialized in the physical sciences, not biology."

"Just a second," Shelby said. She'd finally found the cabinet marked "Woo." She placed the box on the cabinet and tried to go back to the exit. But Shelby got turned around and went down the wrong aisle. Then she saw something she couldn't resist.

"What a second," Shelby said.

Angie couldn't believe it. "What now?"

Shelby pointed to two cabinets marked "Pickett." She tried to open the doors, but they were locked. She tried all of the keys on Mike's chain, but none worked.

"Let's go," Angie insisted. "I don't like it in here."

"I just want to get a peek inside," Shelby replied.

Shelby set the keys down and tried to pull on the edge of the door. It seemed to be budging, when they heard footsteps.

"I bet it's Pickett," Angie whispered.

Angie hid around the end of the shelves and Shelby crawled under a desk. From her vantage point, Shelby could see the person approaching. It was Pickett. He walked up to one of his cabinets and unlocked it. Shelby couldn't see what he was taking from the cabinet. But she did see that he slipped it inside a velvet pouch. It could have been the magnifying glass, but there was no way to tell.

Angie, meanwhile, was about to pass out. Her heart was racing and sweat poured down her face. She didn't like any of it.

Pickett locked his cabinet and started to leave. But then he kicked something on the floor. It was Mike's set of keys. Shelby had left them there. She couldn't believe it.

Pickett picked up the keys and examined them. Then he put them in his pocket and walked away.

Angie was relieved. But just for a second. She didn't know what Shelby knew. She didn't realize yet that they were locked in.

Chapter
5

The moment Lance Pickett was out of sight, Shelby and Angie rushed to the exit. Shelby grabbed the cage door and rattled it. It was locked automatically and the only way to open it was with a key.

Angie began to feel claustrophobic. "This can't be happening," she moaned.

"We'll find a way out," Shelby assured her. "Just stay calm."

"Calm?" Angie cried. "I'm locked in a cage with skulls. How can I be calm? Think about it, Shelby. Maybe these skulls were never forensic evidence. Maybe they are the skulls of people who accidentally got locked in here. I don't want to be a display in an Introduction to Pathology class."

There was no stopping Angie when she got on one of her runs. "Get the skulls out of your mind," Shelby insisted. "You need to think about something else. Let's change the subject."

"You know, there's not a thing you could say that would make me think about anything but those skulls!" Angie insisted.

Shelby sat quietly for a moment. The situation was bleak. They were trapped. The office was closed until Monday. And they couldn't get to a phone. To top it off, Angie was about to freak. Shelby knew she needed to calm her first, but she didn't know how. Then came the idea.

"It *was* a date," Shelby said as if it were a major announcement.

"What are you talking about?" Angie gasped.

"Last night. With Vince," Shelby mumbled. "It was a date."

For a moment at least, Angie forgot all about the dusty skulls.

"I thought you said it wasn't," she demanded.

"Well, I didn't realize it," Shelby explained. "Not until it was over."

"How could you realize it after it was over?"

"When he walked away," Shelby said, "I heard him wonder aloud what the second date might be like. So, I guess he thought last night was the first date."

Angie couldn't hold back her smile. Then it suddenly disappeared. "Why is now the first I'm hearing of this?"

"Well, I was saving it," Shelby replied.

"For what?" asked Angie.

"Until . . . we . . . got locked in a cage with a bunch of skulls. And, it's a good thing I did, 'cause here we are."

Angie stared at her for a moment. Then they both laughed.

"I think you're still holding out crucial info, Woo." Angie wagged a finger at Shelby. Then she considered the situation. "But I'll let it slide until we get out of here. So how do we do it?"

"I have no idea" was Shelby's lame response.

"That's it." Angie couldn't believe her ears. "Come on, what would Sherlock Holmes do?"

"He would have held on to the keys and not gotten into this jam." Shelby was not being very helpful.

Angie tried to stay upbeat. "Okay, what

would Sherlock Holmes's slightly less intelligent cousin do?"

They tried to open a window, but it was painted shut. Shelby came up with the idea of climbing out through the ceiling tiles, but those wouldn't budge.

Angie's enthusiasm quickly disappeared. She started obsessing about the skulls again when Shelby remembered something. Every semester, her grandfather did a lecture on how criminals pick locks. As part of the lecture, he did a demonstration.

She went back to his cabinet and found a box marked locks. Inside the box was a ton of picks and skeleton keys. They were back in business. After about thirty minutes, Shelby finally was able to get the door to swing open.

They made it to the video store just before Angie's shift started. Shelby figured she'd relax the rest of the night and grabbed a Humphrey Bogart movie to watch with her grandfather. Then she walked home.

Even with the cold, Shelby tried to walk as often as she could in Wilton. (Besides, the video store was pretty close.) She thought walking was the best way to learn a new city. You miss so much when you're driving or riding in a car.

Shelby looked for clues in everything. She was always trying to figure out the pattern or puzzle. Like everything else in Wilton, the streets had names that celebrated the American Revolution. But Shelby also noticed that the streets—Adams Avenue, Bunker Hill Place, Constitution Boulevard—were alphabetical.

Shelby thought the Revolutionary names were kind of funny because they were everywhere. She understood the need of an area to celebrate its history, but during her short walk from the video store she passed "The Sons of Liberty Cafe," "Redcoat Cleaners," and an upscale restaurant called "1776."

It's like studying for a history test, Shelby thought. Maybe I'll just walk around before my next big exam.

Mike had resisted the urge to give the bed and breakfast a similar name. He called it the "Easterly Breeze" just as he had the one in Florida. He even uprooted the sign from the other one and placed it in their new front yard.

"Here's a little history of our own," Shelby said as they planted it in the ground.

Shelby went into the inn. Mike was at the registration desk writing reservations in his new planner.

"You're going to wear that thing out," Shelby said as she walked over to him. "Sorry I missed dinner."

"I left you a plate in the kitchen," Mike said. "If you didn't stop for a hamburger."

"Thanks for the dinner—we didn't have time to stop. I brought home a Humphrey Bogart movie." She put the video on the desk.

"Oooh, *The Big Sleep.* One of my favorites." He smiled. "You know, I've seen this movie about five times and I still can't figure out exactly who does what."

"I'm sure we can crack the case together." Shelby loved watching detective movies with her grandfather. Each was a springboard for him to talk about the exciting cases he worked on when he was a criminologist with the San Francisco Police Department.

"By the way, Lance Pickett stopped by," Mike said. "He's the professor who wrote that biography on Allan Pinkerton." Shelby was stunned. A suspect had come to her own home.

"Just to visit?" Shelby couldn't figure out why.

"He brought these." Mike held up the keys. "He found them in the storage room." Shelby was relieved.

"There they are." Shelby was relieved. "I must have dropped them when I put your box back there. Angie and I looked all over for them. I forgot to mention it."

"That's what I figured," Mike replied. "Then I remembered that you can't get through that door without a key."

Busted. Shelby's mind started to race.

"How could you lose them inside the storage room?" Mike wondered aloud.

Shelby tried to think of an explanation. She started to speak, but then thought better of it. She didn't have an answer.

"Maybe while I try to figure out *The Big Sleep*," Mike offered, "you can figure out the right answer."

He headed for the VCR and she went into the kitchen. Shelby didn't know what to tell her grandfather. She hadn't really done anything wrong. Except for going into Pickett's office, but that didn't have anything to do with losing the keys.

Shelby refused to lie to her grandfather. He was too good to her. But she didn't always fill him in on every detail of her mysteries. He was protective and would worry too much. Besides, Shelby was confident she'd never do anything truly dangerous.

She put the dinner plate into the microwave and started to heat it up. She heard her grandfather call out from the other room, "Shelby, you've got a visitor."

She looked up as Vince walked into the kitchen. "Sorry to drop in unexpectedly like this," he said with a shrug. "Did you have a good day?"

Shelby realized that she hadn't seen or called Vince all day. It was pretty rude considering all that had happened the previous evening.

"It was okay," Shelby replied. "Mostly just unpacking boxes. Nothing too exciting."

Vince paused for a moment. "I thought you might call today." Vince searched for the right words. "When I didn't hear from you, I worried you were upset about the car thing. I hope you don't think I was reckless."

"No," Shelby assured him. "Not at all."

I'm not proud of it. But I couldn't tell Vince the truth. I couldn't tell him that I didn't call because I was jealous that he won Detective of the Year. I couldn't tell him that I didn't want him around so that I'd be able to solve the mystery on my own or with Angie.

"Well, I just wanted to make sure." Vince paused for a moment. "I'll let you eat your dinner."

"No," Shelby insisted. "My grandpa and I are going to watch *The Big Sleep*. It stars Humphrey Bogart. Wanna watch it with us?"

"That's a family t-thing," Vince stammered. "I wouldn't want to intrude."

Shelby smirked. "Please." She called out to her grandfather. "You mind if Vince watches the movie with us?"

"Not as long as he knows not to touch my popcorn," Mike called back.

Vince smiled. "I won't."

Shelby went to the cupboard and pulled out a pair of popcorn bags. "We'll play it safe and make two." Vince was in much better spirits.

"Oh, I forgot to tell you," he dragged it out to build excitement. "I got an interesting call today."

"From whom?" Shelby asked.

Vince took a dramatic pause before giving the answer. "Mary Longstreet, president of the Sherlock Society. She said it's urgent for me to go to her office tomorrow."

Chapter 6

Although Vince was being overly dramatic to tease her, Shelby was still concerned about the call. After all, someone had tried to run them off the road the previous night. As long as Mary Longstreet was a suspect, Shelby had to consider her dangerous.

Mary called Vince because she was the publisher of a mystery magazine called *Eureka!* She wanted to get some pictures of him and write an article about his winning the contest at the Mystery Ball. In all the excitement at the museum, she hadn't gotten the chance to do it.

Shelby and Vince went back into the front room to watch the movie with her grandfather.

"Why does she want you to come in on a Sunday?" Shelby wondered. "Don't most magazines work weekdays."

"She said she's facing a deadline and is way behind because she spent so much time organizing the Mystery Ball," Vince explained. "I figured you might want to go with me. Maybe while she's busy talking to me, you can snoop around a little."

"Definitely." Shelby set a bowl of popcorn down by her grandfather. She and Vince took the other one and sat on the couch. Wow, Shelby thought. Dinner and dancing one night, a movie the next.

The next morning Shelby was awakened by the ringing of her telephone. It was Detective Delancey. Shelby could tell by the way her voice crackled that she was using her cell phone. "Shelby, I was wondering if you wouldn't mind meeting me down at the museum," she asked.

Usually Shelby had to sneak into crime scenes. Sometimes she pretended to be passing by. Other times she just lurked around behind the police officers, trying not to draw attention to herself. But she always had to come up with some excuse and she was running out of good ones. That's why she was so excited about this call. If anyone asked, she could say she had been invited.

Shelby hopped out of bed, jumped into the shower, and was through the door in less than ten minutes. She wanted to get out quickly before Detective Delancey had a chance to change her mind and call her back.

Shelby rapped on the glass door of the museum.

"We're closed until noon," boomed the guard.

"I'm supposed to meet with Detective Delancey." Shelby tried to turn her head so she could speak better through the crack between the doors. "I'm Shelby Woo." She said it as if it really meant something important.

The guard scanned a list on a clipboard and saw Shelby's name. He let her in and led her to the third floor. There Sharon Delancey was absently twisting her hair around her finger, her telltale sign of deep thinking.

Delancey was everything Shelby wanted to be in a detective. She was smart and open to fresh approaches. She also cared deeply about the cases to which she was assigned. Delancey's father had been a cop and she used to ride along in his squad car. Now, she had taken Shelby under her wing. She was a good teacher, in part because she didn't just tell Shelby everything— she made her figure a lot of things out for herself.

Shelby stood there for almost a minute before Delancey broke her train of thought and looked up.

"Hi, Shelby, how are you today?" She said it with a smile, but her eyes were still in a heavy haze of confusion.

"Good. How can I help?"

"We've searched every inch of this museum and haven't turned up the slightest clue as to where the magnifying glass is hidden." This was really eating at the detective. "But, I know no one was able to take it out. So, I must be missing something. I want you to walk me through the museum and show me everything that happened that night."

"Sure," said Shelby.

Delancey launched right into it. "Okay, so you arrive with you boyfriend—"

"Just friend," corrected Shelby.

"Too bad. I like him," Delancey continued. "Okay, so you arrive with your just friend. Then what?"

Shelby started to fill her in on the evening, when the guard interrupted them.

"Detective Delancey, we have a problem in the lobby. It's Everett Hood again."

Shelby's ears perked up. Everett Hood was the rich guy who got into the two arguments with Mary Longstreet at the Mystery Ball.

"What does he want now?" Delancey was exasperated. "Didn't you give him back his roses?"

"That's what he wants to talk to you about," said the guard.

"I'm sorry, Shelby." Detective Delancey headed for the stairs. "I'll be right back."

Delancey and the guard went down the main staircase. After a few moments Shelby followed behind. She wanted to hear what Everett Hood was so upset about. Shelby hid in a spot in the stairwell that kept her out of their view but let her see what was going on.

"What happened to my roses?" Hood demanded. He stood next to a line of beautiful pink-and-white rosebushes. They were the ones that had been arranged flanking the entrance.

"I don't know what you mean, Mr. Hood. They're all here," said Delancey.

"They've been mutilated!" Hood was incensed. He waved his cane while he talked. "Someone's dug through the pots."

"Yes, sir." Delancey tried to calm him. "We had to check them to make sure that no one hid the magnifying glass in the soil."

Shelby was impressed—they really had checked everything. She would have never thought of checking the pots. She thought Hood was being ridiculous because the flowers looked perfect to her.

"These are extremely rare and delicate roses," Hood roared. "They probably won't survive now."

"You can file a report and we'll look into replacing the flowers if they don't make it." Delancey was at the end of her rope. "That's the best I can do."

"Replace?!" Hood wouldn't give up. "I spent years cultivating these in my greenhouse. You don't understand. They don't exist anywhere else! They can't be replaced!"

"No, sir." Delancey closed the argument. "You don't understand. I've got a case to solve."

She gave Hood her card and headed back up the steps. Shelby didn't have time to get out of the way. Delancey was sure to catch her.

"Good spot," Delancey said as she checked out Shelby's vantage point. "Could you hear everything?"

"Yes," Shelby replied meekly.

"Come on." Delancey took the stairs two at a time. "Let's solve this thing."

Shelby took Delancey everywhere she'd been that night. They searched all through the exhibit hall and checked out the stairs to get to the terrace. They searched through the cafeteria. Delancey called Shelby's decision to sit by the hot chocolate machine "a stroke of genius."

Finally they went out onto the terrace.

"And this is where I came in," Delancey said, referring to her arrival. "How long were you out here before I got here?"

Shelby thought for a moment. "About forty minutes."

The view from the terrace was magnificent. The balcony was set over a frozen lake that glistened in the sunlight. Delancey breathed in the fresh air. It rejuvenated her.

"I grew up right over there," she said, pointing at a subdivision across the lake.

"Is that where you learned to play field hockey?" Shelby teased.

Delancey shook her head. "Have you been looking at yearbooks again?"

This was an ongoing thing for the two of them. Shelby considered her primary case to be the search for information on the life and times of Sharon Delancey. Her most fruitful discovery had been a collection of old yearbooks she found in the school library.

Shelby started listing off some of what she had uncovered about Delancey. "Sharon Delancey: Field Hockey, School Paper, Police Explorers, and—surprise—Drama Club." This last bit of information had caught Shelby completely off guard.

"Did you see a picture of the guy who starred in all the plays?" Delancey asked. "He was cute."

"How cute?"

"Cute enough for me to join the drama club." Delancey laughed.

Shelby had saved the best for last. "My favorite, though, was your senior quote." Delancey couldn't remember it, but she knew it would be awful. "We will rock you!" Shelby could barely contain her laughter.

"It was a very big song in my youth." Now both of them were laughing. The trip down memory lane had cheered Delancey up, which was exactly why Shelby had brought it all up. The two of them stared out over the city.

"It's pretty," Shelby said.

"Yeah," Delancey replied. "But pretty cold."

Shelby went down to the lobby of the museum. Vince was supposed to pick her up in a few minutes. While she waited, Shelby thought about the case. Hood's tirade made him seem like a fool, but she couldn't figure out if it fit in with the missing magnifying glass.

And she still wasn't sure what she thought about Pickett. That was when she remembered the phone number she had copied from his desk calendar was in her wallet.

She had planned to look it up in the reverse index at the police station. It had all the area phone numbers listed in numerical order. That way, you could look up a number and find out whose it was. But she wouldn't be going into the station until Monday. She went over to the pay phone and dialed.

"Hello," said the woman on the other end.

"Can I speak to Hubert?" Shelby asked, disguising her voice.

"I'm sorry, there's no Hubert here," she replied.

"Are you sure? This is where Hubert told me to call him." Shelby was trying to get her to say who she was.

"I'm positive. This is an antique shop." The woman was getting exasperated.

"Right," Shelby kept up. "Hubert works at an antique shop."

"Well, he doesn't work at Tanney's Antiques," came the response.

Shelby had all she needed. "Then I must have the wrong number. Sorry." Shelby hung up the phone and looked up the address for Tanney's Antiques in the Yellow Pages. She saw Vince pull up in front of the museum.

Vince didn't want to admit why he was running late. But, Shelby finally got him to cough it up. He had put on three different outfits before settling on one that would do.

"It's not often someone takes my picture for a magazine," he explained. He was blushing, which made the experience that much more fun for Shelby.

Vince's dreams of glossy pictures in a slick magazine were dashed the moment they arrived at the humble offices of Eureka! Publishing.

"Thank you so much for coming down here on such short notice," Mary said, greeting them at the door. "In all of the craziness last night, I forgot to get your picture and ask you a few basic questions for the accompanying article."

The offices were actually little more than a big room with two desks. One was reserved for the inner workings of *Eureka!* magazine and the other for those of The Sherlock Society. Giant mounds of paper made a bridge across the floor from one desk to the other.

"Where's the photographer?" Vince asked.

"You're looking at her." Mary laughed. "*Eureka!* magazine is kind of a bare-bones operation. I'm the publisher, editor, writer, and photographer. I also sell the ads."

"You do all that and run the Sherlock Society?" asked Shelby. "That's a lot of work."

"It wasn't supposed to be that way." This was obviously a sore point for her. "I had a big investor set to publish the magazine and I was going to hire a full staff. Unfortunately, that all fell through. And, after last night, I may lose the Sherlock Society as well."

Mary posed Vince up against a colored backdrop she pulled down from the ceiling. She took out her camera and started snapping pictures.

Shelby decided to push it a little. "What happened with the investor?" Vince gave her a look, but Mary was pretty open.

"It all started when I ran for president of the Sherlock Society," she explained. "At the last minute my investor decided *he* wanted to be the president. He didn't like some of the new directions I wanted to take the group. When I won the election, he pulled his support from the magazine."

"That's mature," Shelby said sarcastically.

"Well," said Mary, "no one ever accused Everett Hood of being a grown-up."

Everett Hood. Now things were beginning to make sense to Shelby. That's why they had argued at the Mystery Ball.

"That's it for the pictures," Mary announced. "Let me ask you a few questions and you can get out of here."

Mary pulled out a little tape player and pressed the record button.

7 4

"I'll just go over there and get out of your way," Shelby said. She went to the far side of the room. She had to be careful, but she could still look at what was on the desks.

Shelby picked up a copy of the magazine. It wasn't fancy, but it was good. She also noticed a stack of brochures. She remembered seeing them on the registration table at the Mystery Ball. Shelby picked one up. It was a business proposal for prospective investors.

Everett Hood may have backed out, but Mary obviously hadn't given up. Shelby was beginning to like her. A few minutes later Mary ended the interview.

"Sorry to be so abrupt," she said, "but, I've got a million errands to run."

"Would it be okay if I took one of these magazines and brochures?" Shelby asked.

"Sure. It'd even be okay if you found someone to invest in the magazine." Mary smiled and searched the desk for things she needed. She noticed a stack of flyers. "I better drop these newsletters off in the mailbox today. I probably won't get a chance tomorrow."

Shelby saw a golden opportunity. "We'll take care of those," she offered.

Mary was relieved to have any help. "Really? That'd be great."

Shelby and Vince took the newsletters and left through the front door. Mary locked it behind them and then exited through the rear of the building.

Once they were in Vince's car, Shelby started to sort through the newsletters. Shelby pulled one out. "Ooh, this one's mine. We'll mail it anyway. I love to get mail."

"What are you doing?" Vince asked.

"Looking for this," answered Shelby. She held up a newsletter. On the front of it was Everett Hood's address.

"We can go now," Shelby announced, pleased with herself. Vince started to pull out, but had to slam on the brakes as Mary Longstreet pulled out from the rear driveway.

She was driving a dark-blue Jeep.

It took a moment to dawn on them. Shelby turned to Vince. "Is that the same kind of jeep that forced us off the road?"

"It could be," said Vince. He watched Mary drive down the street and tried to compare it to his memory of the chase. "It certainly could be."

Chapter
7

Shelby reached over her head and kept a tight grip on the strap that dangled from the ceiling of the subway car. She was trying to keep her balance as they rattled under the Charles River. They were about to arrive at the next station and she had to make a decision fast. She scanned the crowd at the other end of the train and looked for clues. She didn't have much to go on.

"Blue shirt," she whispered to Vince and Angie.

"Brown backpack," said Angie.

Vince's eyes darted back and forth before he chimed in with, "Red high-tops."

11

The subway screeched to a stop and the doors *whooshed* open. The man in the blue shirt and the teenager with the brown backpack both got off the train. One point each for Shelby and Angie. Vince wasn't as fortunate. The kid in the red high-tops stood up, but only to get a better seat.

They were playing what Vince and Angie affectionately called "The Shelby Game." It started because Shelby liked to practice her detection skills whenever she rode the subway. The rules were simple. Using nothing but visual clues, each of them picked one passenger they thought would exit at the next stop.

Sometimes it was easy. Lawyer types were always safe bets when you were close to the courthouse. The same went for students cramming for tests anywhere around Harvard and M.I.T. But other times it took more subtle means of deduction.

Shelby had picked the man in the blue shirt because she saw the corner of a tourist map sticking out of his pocket. That particular station was close to the historic Freedom Trail, the most popular tourist spot in town.

Shelby loved the subway and not just because

she got to play this game. She loved it because she didn't have a car. In Cocoa Beach, she always bummed rides off Cindi and Noah, but now all she needed was an eighty-five-cent token and the "T" would take her anywhere. (The "T" is what locals called the mishmash of trains, subways, and trolleys that run throughout the Boston metropolitan area.)

The trio got off at ancient Park Street Station—the very first subway station in America. Shelby liked the street musicians who played funky music on the platform. Her favorite was a kid who played drums on a bucket. She also liked the giant mural of Boston made of everything from ceramic to horseshoes to railroad spikes.

They stepped out onto the street and Shelby breathed in the aroma of all the street vendors. It brought an instant smile to her face. The were right at Boston Common, one of the most famous parks in the country.

"So what's this guy's story?" Angie asked as they began to walk toward the exclusive Back Bay section of town.

"You mean other than the fact that he's some flower freak who walks with a cane for no apparent reason and threw a major hissy fit when he didn't get elected president of the Sherlock Society?" Shelby asked rhetorically.

"Yeah," Angie said. "Like is there anything unusual about him?"

Shelby was amazed by the giant mansions that lined Commonwealth Avenue. They were walking down a mall of trees and statues that formed a mile-long park that split the two lanes of traffic on the street.

"How rich *is* this guy?" Shelby asked when they reached the address that matched the one on the newsletter. They were standing in front of a gigantic Victorian mansion that sat back beautifully behind the snow-covered lawn.

Vince was apprehensive as he pushed the doorbell. It produced a loud bellow. "It's got to be that loud just so they can hear it all the way in the back," he said only half-joking. After a few moments, they heard the approaching footsteps of Everett Hood's butler.

"Yes?" he questioned in a deep distinctive voice as he opened the door.

"We're here to see Everett Hood," Shelby ventured.

They could tell the butler didn't believe them. "It's a pressing business matter," Vince offered lamely.

If he wasn't a stern-faced butler, he would have laughed at the idea of three teenagers having "pressing business" with Everett Hood. Instead, he just asked, "Regarding?"

Doesn't this guy ever put two words together? Vince thought.

"The Sherlock Society," said Shelby.

The butler considered this for a moment. His boss took everything about the Sherlock Society seriously. "The greenhouse." He pointed around the side of the mansion.

Two words, Vince thought. We must be growing on him.

As they walked to the greenhouse, Vince couldn't help but notice a four-car garage at the back of the property. The car lover in him wondered what expensive automobiles Hood might have in there. The detective, however, was only interested to see if one of them was a dark-colored Jeep.

Shelby rapped against the door to the greenhouse. Inside they could make out Everett Hood. Having seen him with Detective Delancey,

Shelby was ready for him to start yelling. But, quite the contrary, he couldn't have been friendlier.

"I know you. You won Detective of the Year." He pumped Vince's hand. "I won it a few times myself. Good show, young man! Good show!"

Shelby once again felt the tinge of jealousy.

"Come in and get warm," Hood continued. "Who are these nice young ladies?"

Shelby and Angie introduced themselves and they all went into the greenhouse. Shelby couldn't believe it. Even though it was freezing outside, inside it felt like Florida in July.

"These are unbelievable!" Angie was overwhelmed by the rows and rows of beautiful roses. Shelby and Vince were equally impressed. The roses gradually changed in shades from white to dark red as they went across the greenhouse. The entire place was filled with a wondrous fragrance.

"They're everything to me," Hood said. "Them and the Sherlock Society. Please come over here. I'm trying to rescue some." He motioned with his cane for them to follow.

He led them to the flowers Shelby had seen him pick up at the museum. The petals were a blend of red, white and pink. No two roses were the same.

"These are hybrids," Angie said as she examined them. Vince and Shelby were lost. "I studied these in botany. You've crossbred all the other roses to make an entirely new one."

"That's right," he said with a smile. "It's taken me decades. There's nothing like them in the world. I have rich soil specially brought to me from Costa Rica. That's my secret."

"What did you name them?" asked Angie. Angie thought that was the best perk of scientific discovery. If you were the first to see or do something, you got to name it.

"I call them Doyle's Delight," he informed her, "because they're filled with mystery."

Shelby thought about this for a minute. Then it dawned on her. "After Arthur Conan Doyle," she said. "The creator of Sherlock Holmes."

"Three bright young souls. This is refreshing," he told them.

"Why did you say they need rescuing?" Angie was growing concerned for the beautiful flowers.

"They were manhandled at the Mystery Ball

over the weekend," he explained. "I should have known better, but I wanted to do something to cheer up that wretched party. I guess I should feel lucky they weren't stolen."

"I thought it was a fun party," Vince said.

"Of course," Hood agreed. "But is fun what we should be about? Besides, it was just so poorly orchestrated. Who ever heard of dancing on the terrace in the middle of winter?"

You've got a point there, Shelby thought.

"And then that dreadful crime." He was nearly seething. "This organization, which my grandfather began over sixty years ago, may never recover its good name. Two nights ago was just another in a string of inept things that woman has done to destroy it."

That's why he's so concerned about it, Shelby realized. Because his grandfather started it.

Hood quickly composed himself. "Anyway, it certainly has nothing to do with you fine young people. To what do I owe the honor of your visit?"

Shelby groped for a quick excuse. Then she dug into her pocket and pulled out the newsletter. "We just wanted to deliver this." She handed it to him.

"Typical mismanagement," he said shaking his head. "Three people to deliver a newsletter."

They let him resume his work and exited back into the freezing cold. Vince paid close attention to find a spot out of view from the greenhouse and the mansion.

"Keep on walking," Vince said as he stopped in his tracks.

"What are you doing?" asked Shelby.

He motioned over to the garage. "I want to look for a certain car," he explained.

"What?" Angie demanded. "You think that nice old man is guilty?"

"I'll think he's a lot nicer if I don't see a dark Jeep in there." Vince bent low and hurried as fast as he could across the lawn. He could only hope that the butler was nowhere nearby.

Shelby and Angie continued out to the street. They had to get out of sight quickly so no one would notice they were missing a person.

Vince went around to the back of the garage because there was too much risk of being caught if he stayed in front. He found a secluded spot and tried to climb up to peer in through a window.

He planted his foot on a brick and pulled himself up by the sill. The brick was icy, and his foot slid out from under him. He went crashing facedown into the snow. He had started to brush himself off when he heard it. It was a low growl. He looked up and found himself face to face with a snarling Doberman pinscher.

Chapter
8

The Doberman bared its teeth inches from Vince's face. Vince could see its breath in the cold air and didn't know what to do. He was certain if he made the slightest movement, the dog would bite his nose off. He was also pretty certain it would do that even if he didn't move. He tried to say, "Nice doggie," but he couldn't get the words to come out.

"What are you doing?" It was the distinctive voice of Hood's butler. Vince was afraid to answer. He motioned to the dog with his eyes. "Sit, Cupid," the butler commanded and the dog instantly sat, the snarl an ancient memory on his face.

Cupid? Vince couldn't believe this life-threatening beast had such a name. He stood up and wiped the snow off his chest.

"Now, what were you doing?" The butler was not in a mood to wait. Vince looked around desperately. Then he saw a garbage can.

"I was heading for that," he said, pointing at the can, "when I slipped and Cupid here tried to put an arrow right through my heart."

"The garbage?" The butler was back to two-word sentences.

"Yes," Vince insisted. "I found this on the ground." He reached into his pocket and pulled out an empty gum wrapper. "This place is beautiful. I had to get rid of it."

The butler considered the gum wrapper and Vince saw his opening. "Who's supposed to keep this place clean, by the way?"

The butler instantly demurred and offered to take the wrapper. Vince insisted he throw it away himself. He walked over to the garbage can hoping he'd get a glimpse inside the garage. He couldn't. Still, he very dramatically lifted the lid and threw the trash into the can. Vince didn't want to push his luck. He walked up the driveway and got away as fast as he could.

Sometimes when I walk through the cafeteria at school, I feel like a total alien. The place looks like a meeting room for some kind of high-school United Nations. At one table is the delegation from Jock World. At another are the ambassadors from Brainland. Don't get me started on the kids who feel the need to pierce everything. In fact, it seems like every group has its own table except one—me and my friends.

I've never really felt like I belong in any of those groups, although I've had friends in most. It used to bother me that I'd didn't fit in. Now, I'm kind of glad I don't. Anyway, I usually eat with Vince and Angie out on the patio—if it's warm enough. Sometimes even if it isn't.

Shelby hurried across the patio toward Angie. "Did you know about that American lit test?" Shelby asked desperately as she took her spot on the bench.

"Sure. Mrs. White announced it on Thursday," Angie said. "Didn't you study?"

"No." Shelby couldn't believe it. "I think I bombed. Who wrote that thing about living out in the woods? Emerson?"

"Thoreau," Angie answered. "It was called *Walden.*"

Shelby cringed. She resigned herself to the fact she didn't do well on the test and made a noise like a bomb falling from an airplane and exploding on impact.

Vince came rushing up with his bag lunch. He started in on the test before he even sat down. "Please tell me that was *Walden.* By Henry David Thoreau." He anxiously looked to Angie for confirmation.

"Yes," she said, bringing him instant relief.

"At least I got one right." Vince plopped down on the bench. "Tests should not be allowed on Mondays."

"Did you study?" Shelby was incredulous.

"No. I forgot," Vince admitted.

"Then how did you know that answer?"

"He wrote it at Walden Pond," explained Vince. "That's not far from here."

"Ah-ha." Shelby seized the moment. "The test was prejudiced against people who just moved here." Vince and Angie rolled their eyes.

"No," said Angie. "It's just prejudiced against people who didn't study."

Shelby flashed Angie a mean look, but knew

she was right. Still, she couldn't afford a bad test grade.

"You could recite a poem in class for extra credit," Vince offered.

"No way," Shelby said shaking her head. "I can't talk in front of strangers."

"Strangers?" Vince was amazed. "They're your classmates. Some of them have names."

"That's even worse than strangers," Shelby declared.

"Get this girl," said Angie. "She'll burst right into a crime scene, but she's scared to recite Robert Frost to a classroom of kids who aren't even paying attention."

"I'm complex," Shelby offered in self-defense.

Vince dug into his bag to look for some sugar concoction to start his meal. "Uh-oh."

"What's the matter? Nothing good in there?" Shelby asked.

"No," Vince said. "Nothing good over there."

He motioned across the patio to Christie Sayers, who was heading straight for their group. All of them sagged in their seats.

"I think it's morally wrong for someone to hate another person," Angie announced to the other two. "But if you got to pick just one, that'd be my girl."

The rap sheet against Christie was pretty extensive. She was your best friend when she needed something. And she treated you like a total stranger when she didn't. She did well in school, which was all right, but she rubbed it in everybody's face, which wasn't.

Since they didn't run in the popular crowd, it should have been easy for them to avoid Christie. Except there was a problem. Christie wanted to solve mysteries. It was one in a series of desperate pleas for attention. This made her ultra-competitive with Shelby.

"You hear what happened at the museum this weekend?" Christie asked, fishing for information. They all played dumb.

"What museum?" asked Shelby.

Christie wasn't buying it. "The Museum of History. Someone stole a priceless glass that belonged to Abraham Lincoln."

Magnifying glass, thought Shelby. And it was a gift from Lincoln. She can't even get the crime right.

"Pretty stupid," Vince replied. "Who'd want some old glass?"

Now Christie wasn't sure. She was certain they would have read about it in the paper. But then again, maybe they didn't know anything about it.

Shelby sensed her apprehension. "Wow, guys, maybe we should look into it." Shelby turned to the others. "What can you tell us about it, Christie?"

Christie had come looking for information. She didn't want to give any. "Just what I read in the paper." She tried to change the subject. "How about that English test? Talk about easy. What a joke."

That was it for Shelby. She wanted Christie gone. "After school why don't we go down to the museum and see what we can find?"

"It's closed on Mondays," Christie reminded them. "Besides, the police will probably have it solved by tomorrow. Gotta go."

Christie hurried back across the patio. Once she was gone, Vince tried to shake off what he called "Residual Christie Crusties."

"Christie would die if she knew Delancey took you through the museum yesterday," said Vince. He thought for a moment. "Maybe I should tell her."

"Let her spend her time at the museum," Shelby said. "I don't think the answer's there."

"Then where?" wondered Angie.

"Maybe Tanney's Antiques. We know that Pickett went into work the morning after the crime even though it was a Saturday," Shelby reasoned. "And he wrote down Tanney's number that day on his calendar. We've got to figure out why. Let's go today. Who's with me?"

"I can't," Vince answered. "My brother's going to help me work on my car."

"Then I guess that leaves us," Shelby said as she put an arm around Angie.

"I'm not going," Angie replied firmly as she took Shelby's arm off her shoulder. "I got locked in a room with skulls the last time I went somewhere with you."

"Really," Vince added. "I almost got eaten by a Doberman."

"Come on," Shelby pleaded. "What can happen at an antique shop? Besides, it'll take at least two of us to pull it off."

"No." Angie was resistant.

"You'll get to play a part," Shelby tempted. Angie loved it when they pretended to be other people. Angie mulled this over in her head for a minute.

"Okay, I'll do it," she said. "But on one condition."

"Anything." Shelby smiled and mentally started to plot their way into Tanney's.

"You recite a poem in Mrs. White's class," replied Angie.

Shelby's planning stopped cold. "No way," she cried. "That's not fair."

"You need to bring your grade up," Angie told her. "And to do that, you need extra credit."

"Why do you care about my grade?" wondered Shelby.

"I care because if your grades drop, you'll get restricted," Angie said. "And if *you* get put on restriction, *my* social life will suffer. And then, maybe, I won't meet the right guy because of it. Next thing, I'm some ancient, never-been-married scientist staring at a petri dish wondering why my life's so empty."

Shelby and Vince shared a look. "You went from my bombing a test to your having an empty, loveless life," said Shelby. "That's pretty out there, Ang."

"Complex," Angie corrected. "I can be complex, too."

Shelby didn't like the arrangement, but she agreed to it. She would recite a poem in class for extra credit and Angie would help her at Tanney's. She'd worry about the stage fright later.

Tanney's was one of many antique shops and upscale boutiques in Wilton's historic district. Shelby knew she wouldn't find Pinkerton's magnifying glass just sitting on display, but it was still worth checking. If Angie could distract the shopkeeper long enough, maybe Shelby could find some clue as to why Professor Pickett had called.

Shelby was amazed at Angie's transformation. With just a couple of accessories from her closet—scarf, sunglasses, and necklace—the mild-mannered, brilliant science girl had become the obnoxious, stinking-rich spoiled girl. It was the perfect character.

Angie went into the antique shop first. She went directly to the woman at the counter and dramatically extended her hand.

"Bootsy Van Der Kellen of the Newport Van

Der Kellens," she said, introducing herself with the snobbiest name that came to mind. The woman had no choice but to take her hand. "My father is Nelly Van Der Kellen, whom I'm sure you've heard of. Anyway, last month Daddy and Uncle Tad got into a horrible argument and long story short, they disbanded the company."

Shelby slipped into the store and pretended to look at some knickknacks in the corner.

"That's very interesting," said the woman, "but why are you telling me this?"

"Don't you see?" Angie said. "Grandma is furious. She's written both of them out of her will and has decided to sell all of the antiques. Even the ones at the English estate. We're talking major commission for whoever oversees the sale."

Suddenly the woman was very interested in the story of the Van Der Kellen family. "Let me get my partner," she said.

In a moment Angie was regaling both the woman and her partner with stories of the amazing Van Der Kellen heirlooms. They were much too enthralled in the prospect of riches to notice Shelby slip down the hall into the now vacant office.

Shelby instantly went about searching the desk. If Pickett had called, there might be a memo somewhere. Shelby whipped through a couple dozen phone message slips, but none had Pickett's name. She tried to open a file cabinet, but it was locked.

This is taking too long, she thought. She was worried she'd get caught. There was no way to explain her way out of this. Then she noticed a small daily planner like the one she had given her grandfather.

She picked it up and flipped through the upcoming week's schedule. On Wednesday, she found a four-thirty appointment penciled in for Lance Pickett. And, beneath Pickett's name was written a single word—*Pinkerton*.

Chapter
9

On Wednesday school let out early, giving Shelby, Angie, and Vince extra time to try to crack the case. There were still unanswered questions about each of the suspects. The longer they waited, the colder the trail to the culprit would become. They decided to separate and each follow one of the suspects.

Shelby was going to start at the police station before heading over to Tanney's Antiques. She would be there when Lance Pickett showed up for his four-thirty appointment.

Vince was determined to get a look in Everett

Hood's garage. And, this time, he knew to bring dog treats in case he ran into Cupid.

Angie was left to follow Mary Longstreet. She was the only one who could do it because they had never met. There was too great a risk that Mary would recognize Shelby or Vince if she saw them on the street.

Angie waited across the street from Eureka! Publishing for about twenty minutes before she saw Mary pull out of her driveway. Angie almost lost her immediately because her car was facing the opposite direction. She had to do an illegal U-turn at the first intersection. But she caught up with Mary and was careful to stay a couple cars behind the dark-blue Jeep.

As she tailed the entire staff of *Eureka!* magazine, Angie realized what had initially made her become friends with Shelby. I never did stuff like this before, she thought. I never did totally stupid, dangerous, adventure-girl stuff. Amazingly, this realization brought a smile to her face.

Angie followed the Jeep into the parking lot of Cavanaugh's Market. She waited until Mary got into the store before getting out of her car.

Since Angie didn't know what might be

important later, she made mental notes of every single thing Mary did. By the time Mary reached the cashier, Angie had memorized everything in her cart: loaf of French bread, box of cereal, deli platter, cheddar cheese, three bags of potato chips, two six-packs of soda.

Haven't you heard of fruit? Angie wanted to call out across the store. Mary was obviously planning a party. And, despite the lack of healthy alternatives, the food was making Angie very hungry. Next time, she thought, I'll bring snacks.

When Shelby arrived at the police station, she found a piece of paper on her desk. It was a photocopy of a picture from her Cocoa Beach yearbook. Her grandfather was obviously conspiring with Detective Delancey in the battle of the embarrassing yearbook pictures. As if the yearbook picture wasn't bad enough, Delancey added magic-marker freckles and blacked out one of Shelby's teeth.

Above the picture she had written, "Shelby Woo, where are you?" Shelby realized she hadn't been hanging out at the police station as often as usual the past few days. Delancey knew that meant she was probably getting into trouble.

"Do you know where Detective Delancey is?" Shelby asked the desk sergeant, who was deeply engrossed in a basketball game he was watching on his portable television. He looked at the board behind him. Next to Delancey's name was written Out. He turned back to Shelby. "She's out." He smiled knowing Shelby wouldn't be bothering him again.

Shelby went over to Delancey's desk to leave her a note. She couldn't believe what she saw sitting on top of the endless pile of paper. It was a folder marked "Pinkerton Magnifying Glass— Museum of History."

It was the case file. All Shelby had to do was open it up. She looked around. No one was there but the desk sergeant, and he was glued to his game. She knew she wasn't supposed to look, but it was too good to pass up. Shelby took a breath and opened the file. The only thing in it was another photocopy from her yearbook. Under this picture Delancey had written, "Shelby's duties: Filing, cleaning, errands, and NOT LOOKING IN FILES." Shelby shut the folder. She knew when she was beaten.

*   *   *

Vince bypassed Everett Hood's mansion and went straight for the greenhouse. He'd knock there to see if Hood was inside. If he was nowhere in sight, Vince'd go to the garage and look for a Jeep.

He knocked on the glass. Hood was at the door in an instant, but this time he wasn't smiling. "You again?" Vince couldn't tell how friendly Hood was going to be.

"Yes, sir. I'm sorry to bother you. But I need to ask you a question." Vince sounded hopeful.

"About what?" Hood didn't.

"Roses," Vince said. Hood's demeanor changed ever so slightly and Vince knew he had an entry point. "Specifically, sir, the type of roses a young man might give to . . . well . . . you know, a young girl he likes."

Hood opened the door far enough to let Vince inside the greenhouse. "It's the girl you were with at the Mystery Ball, isn't it?"

"Yes, sir." Vince tried to appeal to his sense of romance. After all, this was a man who named a killer dog Cupid.

"She was particularly taken by a type of rose we saw in here the other day," Vince continued.

"I know yours are rare, but I thought maybe you could tell me what rose like it I could find at a regular florist."

This was a little weird for Vince. He was doing it as a ruse to check out Hood, but he kind of liked the idea that he was getting a rose for Shelby.

"Which rose is it?" Hood asked him.

Vince looked over at the pink ones that he liked the best. "I think it was that one."

"Pink Revelation," said Hood. "She has good taste."

"Yes, she does." Suddenly Vince really wanted the flower.

"I tell you what," Hood said. "That one's not so rare. Let me donate one. Think of it as part of your award for winning the contest."

High on a shelf, there were small pots with newly potted roses. Hood took his cane and slipped its wooden tip into the pot's hanger. The pot slid right down it into his hand.

So, that's what the cane's for, Vince thought.

He handed Vince the flower. Vince was really warming up to him. "You know," he said. "I can really appreciate how important the Sherlock Society is to you. I've got a watch that belonged to my grandfather and it means the world to me."

"Tomorrow afternoon the executive board of the Sherlock Society is holding an emergency meeting at the house," Hood said. "We'll be discussing the immediate dismissal of Mary Longstreet. I have a good feeling that the organization will be able to regain its reputation."

Vince still wasn't sure about this guy, but he was beginning to think he was just harmlessly eccentric.

"Now, I have to get this out to the garbage can." Hood motioned to a small wheelbarrow full of plant debris.

"I'll do it," Vince offered. The garbage can was right by the garage. He could be sure to get a look inside. "You've been so nice to me, it's the least I can do."

Vince didn't even wait for a response. He took the barrow by the handles. He carefully placed the Pink Revelation on top of the pile and noticed a dead rosebush. Vince could identify it by the red, pink, and white petals.

"One of your Doyle's Delights didn't make it."

"Unfortunately, no," Hood replied. "Luckily, the rest are doing fine. The garbage is down this path," Hood said, gesturing toward the garage. "Just leave the wheelbarrow there."

"Yes, sir," Vince answered. "And once again, thank you for the flower."

Vince marveled at how neatly the walkway had been shoveled. It made it easy work to push the wheelbarrow. He was careful to keep a look-out for Cupid. There was no sight of him, but he patted his pocket just to make sure the treats were still there.

Vince dumped the debris in the garbage. He was particularly saddened by the rosebush. He didn't know much about flowers, but he was certain this one was special.

By this point he was certain Hood was inno-cent. Then he looked into the open garage. It held all the fancy cars Vince expected. It also held a jet-black Jeep.

After they left the grocery store, Angie fol-lowed Mary Longstreet to the First Bank of Wil-ton. This stop worried her. It was one thing for a teenager to stand around a grocery store looking hungry. It was quite another for one to be stand-ing around a bank with no money to withdraw or deposit.

Angie tried to act nonchalant. Mary didn't go to a cashier; instead she signed up on a sheet at the receptionist's desk and took a seat. Angie followed suit. She looked at the sheet and saw that in the column "Reason for Visit," Mary had written "New Business Account."

"Are you going to sign in?"

Angie looked up. It was the receptionist. "Are you going to sign in?" she repeated.

"Yes." Angie quickly signed in and gave as a reason, "New Personal Account." Angie smiled at the receptionist and took a seat near, but not too close to, Mary.

A few moments later a banker came over to Mary and led her to his desk. They were too far out of earshot for Angie to hear what was happening. She strained anyway.

"So you want to open an account with us?" Angie heard. But it wasn't the banker talking to Mary. It was a woman talking to Angie.

She spun around to see a very conservatively dressed woman talking to her. "What?" Angie momentarily forgot what she had written. "Yes," she said. "I'd like to open an account."

"Please come this way." The woman led

Angie to her desk. It was just two away from where Mary was feverishly filling out forms.

Angie did her best to act like she was paying attention to the woman giving the sales pitch, while she was actually trying to hear what Mary was saying.

The best that Angie could make out was that Mary was opening a new account for *Eureka!* magazine. She couldn't make out any specifics until the end. That was when she overheard Mary make the initial deposit—a cashier's check for fifty thousand dollars.

Professor Lance Pickett walked into Tanney's Antiques at precisely four-thirty. Shelby was looking at some clocks on the wall closest to the office. She didn't know where the meeting would take place, but her bet was that it would be in the back.

The woman greeted him with a smile and waved him back to the office. Pickett looked a little nervous and Shelby decided to turn up the pressure.

"Professor Pickett?" She walked up to him and pumped his hand. This made him extremely uncomfortable. "How nice to run into you." She noticed that the velvet pouch from the storage room was tucked into his pocket.

"I'm sorry," he said. "But do I know you?"

"Shelby Woo," she reminded him. "My grand-father teaches with you at Grayson College." Now Pickett was visibly agitated. He had wanted this to be a private transaction. Shelby kept it up.

"You know," she continued. "He was just raving about your biography of Allan Pinkerton."

The antique dealer came out from his office to see what was keeping Pickett.

"There you are," he said. "I've been dying to see Pinkerton's pocket watch all week. If it's as good as that other piece you brought in, my client is sure to pay top dollar."

Lance Pickett didn't know how much damage had been done. He just closed his eyes and wished it would all end.

Chapter
10

As she started shoveling snow, Shelby wondered what was going on back in Cocoa Beach. She pictured Cindi and Noah in the warm Florida sun running around in shorts and T-shirts. Or better yet, driving around in Cindi's convertible. Here she was "Shelby of the Great White North."

The cold air whistled across her face. She couldn't figure out the pieces in this puzzle. She took a big scoop of snow and dumped it. Everything about the case was muddled in her mind. Another shovelful and dump. Soon she had a rhythm going. Scoop, lift, toss. It became like a reflex and left her mind open to consider the theft of the magnifying glass.

Right now, the evidence seemed to be pointing at Lance Pickett. But she had trouble believing it was him. After all, Grandpa thought he was a great guy. More than anyone, Shelby trusted her grandfather to be an excellent judge of character.

Vince and Angie both pulled up to Shelby's house at the same time. Each was eager to talk.

"I know who did it," they both told Shelby at once. Then they proceeded to each pick a different person.

It's funny to watch how people think. Angie and Vince go about solving mysteries in opposite ways. Vince is very mechanical. He likes to know how things work. He starts with the idea of figuring out how the crime could have been committed and then tries to figure out who was capable of doing it. Angie, though, works on a mystery like it's a chemistry experiment. She likes to look at all the elements and figure out how they could react with one another.

"It has to be Hood," Vince declared. "Everything points to him. It turns out he does have a

Jeep," he added, "so he could have been the one who followed us and almost got us killed. Plus, he wants Mary Longstreet kicked out of the Sherlock Society and it looks like he may get his wish. Tomorrow the executive board is having an emergency meeting, the topic of which will be Mary's dismissal."

Vince smiled confidently, like a lawyer who just made a masterful closing argument. Everything was perfect. Except the way Shelby was shoveling the snow.

"You're still doing it all wrong," he said. "You need to scoop more and then throw. Let me show you."

Shelby gladly handed the shovel over to Vince, who instantly went to work on the walkway. Angie shook her head. She couldn't believe Vince was falling for this again. Shelby knew perfectly well how to shovel snow, as evidenced by the section she'd already cleared. And he thought of himself as a detective.

"If Mary Longstreet is in such dire trouble," Angie asked, "why does she act like she's about to host a Super Bowl party. I followed her to the grocery store and she bought up half the snack aisle."

"Big deal," said Vince.

"And, I followed her to the First Bank of Wilton," Angie countered. "Where she opened a new business account with a cashier's check for fifty thousand dollars."

Shelby and Vince stopped cold.

"That is a big deal," said Shelby.

"But, she's broke," claimed Vince.

"Doesn't look like it now, shovel boy." Now Angie was the cocky one. "By the way," she added as a point of information, "I'd look into opening a new account down there. They have a lot of great services like unlimited checking and free on-line banking."

"Now I'm confused," muttered Shelby. "Because I was certain Lance Pickett was guilty. I saw him sell Allan Pinkerton's pocket watch at Tanney's Antiques. The antique dealer mentioned having bought a similar piece from him earlier in the week."

"So they're all guilty," Angie joked.

The three of them plopped down into the snow. Each had made a strong argument for guilt. But they couldn't all be right.

"What are we missing?" pondered Shelby.

Vince returned to his mechanical approach.

"Which of them had a chance to grab the magnifying glass?"

"Hood had that argument with Mary Longstreet when we all went to the terrace," remembered Shelby. "If she stormed off, he would have had a few moments alone in the exhibit hall."

"And you said Pickett stayed inside the whole time," offered Angie. "He could easily have slipped back down the stairs and grabbed it."

"And Mary was out of sight sorting through the ballots," added Vince. "So she had plenty of time."

They thought some more. "But none of them could have taken it out," said Shelby. "Each of them was closely searched."

"That's the key," Vince stated. "If we can figure out how the thief got it out of the museum, we can figure out who did it."

He picked up the shovel and started back on the walkway.

"That's it," cried Shelby. "It's just like at the Mystery Ball. Sometimes you look so hard for a really tough clue that you miss the one right in front of you."

114

Vince and Angie look around. "Right in front of you, where?" asked Vince.

"Everywhere," replied Shelby.

Angie and Vince looked around some more, but all they saw was snow.

Shelby explained as they drove over to the museum. "Whoever did it," she said, "used the snow to get the magnifying glass out of the museum. After the mystery, everyone went to the rooftop terrace, which overlooks the lake. Because the ground is covered in snow, all the thief had to do was drop the magnifying glass over the edge and come back for it later."

Angie went over the physics of it all in her head. "It would probably work," she said. "But to be safe, the thief would probably want to wrap something protective around it."

After parking in the museum lot, the three of them headed for the lake. There was no direct access, so they had to make their way through the heavy woods that grew up to the museum on two sides.

Shelby shielded her face from the branches and tried to keep her balance in the snow. Finally they broke through the woods and reached the lake side.

"There!" Shelby pointed to a trail of deep footsteps in a snow bank leading out over the frozen water. The tracks went in a straight line to a point about ten yards out. There the snow was all disturbed. "Whoever it was came back for the glass."

The prospect of finding a clue overcame Shelby. Without the slightest hesitation, she started tromping out to follow the tracks.

"Shelby," called Angie. "You've got to be careful on ice."

"I'll be careful," Shelby called back.

Vince and Angie shared a look.

"This girl's crazy," Angie said.

"I know," Vince replied. "But that's part of her appeal. You know, never a dull moment." Vince started after Shelby. Angie, though, stayed put. She didn't share their adventurous spirit.

Shelby reached the point where the tracks stopped. Someone had dug around in the snow. "This is it!" She turned to Vince and pointed up. "Look."

Vince looked up and sure enough, they were directly under the edge of the overhanging terrace. Shelby started to dig around in the snow, careful to disturb the scene as little as possible.

"Any clues?" asked Vince.

"No. Just a lot of dirt." Shelby was disappointed. Then she saw something bright embedded in the ice. She kneeled down to get it when she heard a sound she had never heard before. It was the sound of ice breaking—directly beneath her.

Chapter
11

As Shelby plunged into the freezing water, she desperately grabbed at the snow to stop her slide. But she couldn't get a grip on anything. The snow and ice just slipped through her fingers. She disappeared completely under the surface and felt a freezing shock like none she'd ever known.

She forced herself back up toward the surface and cut her forehead against the bottom of the ice. The hole was gone. She was trapped under the ice. Remaining calm, she methodically felt around until she found the opening. She lifted her head up and took a deep breath. Vince was waiting for her and grabbed her by the wrist. He lay down against the ice. Shelby could breathe now, but she would soon freeze to death.

"What do I do?" she asked deep in panic, her blue lips quivering.

"Pull yourself up hand over hand, holding on to me. Try not to put too much pressure on any one spot." He remained still and Shelby tried to pull herself up by his arm. But wherever she tried to get a hold, the ice broke. Now she was endangering Vince.

"I'm sorry," Shelby said between chattering teeth. "This is all my fault."

"This?" Vince tried to calm her. "This is nothing. We'll get you out of there in a second." He took a deep breath. "I just don't know how."

Suddenly Angie appeared. Her normal apprehensions disappeared the moment Shelby had disappeared from view. She grabbed a dead tree branch and headed straight for them. She was careful to come at Shelby from a different direction so she wouldn't put any pressure on ice they'd already weakened.

"Take this," she said, holding one end of the branch out to Shelby. Shelby grabbed the branch with a firm grip.

"I've got her," Angie told Vince. "I need you to help me." Vince carefully let go of Shelby's hand once he was certain she had a good grip on the branch. Then he moved over to Angie. Together, the two of them pulled on the branch and in the process lifted Shelby up and out of the water.

An hour later Shelby was sitting on her bed wrapped in a blanket and cupping her hands around a mug of hot tea. She had finally begun to warm up. Angie and Vince had spent most of her thaw time lecturing her on the dangers of frozen lakes. Shelby, though, was more concerned that she had lost the silver object. It had fallen to the bottom of the lake when the ice broke.

"I can't believe I didn't get that thing before it fell into the water. My only clue and I let it get away. We went through all that and we don't even have any evidence to show for it."

Angie would have none of it. "No more mysteries," Angie decreed. "You've got to recover now. And that means you stay in bed and make sure you don't get pneumonia."

"That's fine," said Shelby, "but if I don't think

about the mystery, what am I supposed to do sitting in bed?"

"I'm glad you asked," Angie said with a grin. "Look what I brought." Angie reached into her backpack and pulled out a pair of books.

"What are those?" Shelby asked suspiciously.

"Your homework," said Angie. "We've got to find a poem for you to memorize."

Shelby had forgotten all about the poem. "I don't think so, Angie."

"You promised. Besides, you have to if for no other reason than to get a better grade than Christie Sayers."

Shelby thought about that for a moment. "Okay. What've you got?"

"Mrs. White once said that in college she specialized in New England poets. So I brought a book of Walt Whitman and one of Robert Frost. They'll make for good Brownie points."

Vince got excited. "I know the perfect poem," he said. "Give me the Frost."

Shelby and Angie didn't know what to make of his sudden interest. Vince and poetry? He flipped through the book and stopped when he found the right page.

"Here," said Vince. " 'Stopping by Woods on

a Snowy Evening.' " He handed the book to Shelby. Shelby scanned over it and read the first verse aloud.

Whose woods these are I think I know.
His house is in the village, though;
He will not see me stopping here
To watch his woods fill up with snow.

Shelby looked up. "I like it."

"Vince," said Angie. "That's one of my all-time favorite poems. I didn't know you were into stuff like that."

"What?" Vince protested. "You think I only know about cars and engines."

"I misjudged you," Angie apologized. "I'm sorry."

"Besides," Vince continued, "it rhymes. I had all those poems that don't rhyme."

Angie shook her head. "Maybe I didn't misjudge you."

Shelby looked over the poem. It was only sixteen lines. It couldn't be that hard to remember.

Vince said that once when he had to memorize a poem for class, he learned it by singing it to himself. "The tune made it easier to keep it all straight."

Shelby was willing to try anything that might help. She spent a good part of the night memorizing the poem. But, despite Angie's best intentions for her, she fell asleep trying to figure out who had dropped the magnifying glass from the edge of the terrace.

The next day in class Shelby nervously drummed her fingers against her desk. She ran over the poem in her head again and again. Unfortunately, each time she did, it came out sounding like Vince's silly song. She couldn't get the tune out of her head. Shelby looked over at Vince. She wanted to throttle him.

Vince just gave her the thumbs-up.

"Do we have any recitations for today?" Mrs. White asked from the head of the class. Shelby didn't move. Angie gave her a dirty look, but Shelby still didn't move. Finally, Angie poked her with her pen and Shelby let out a yelp.

"Was that you, Shelby?" asked Mrs. White.

There was no getting out of it. "Yes, ma'am."

"Do you have a poem you'd like to recite?"

"Yes, I do." Shelby stood up and started walking to the front of the class. She was very nervous. "I'm going to recite 'Stopping by the Woods on a Snowy Evening' by Robert Frost."

Mrs. White frowned. "Eeuuh. Probably his worst poem."

Shelby froze in her tracks. Angie had promised Brownie points. Then Mrs. White cackled. "Just kidding. It's wonderful poetry."

Great, thought Shelby. It's not bad enough that I've got to make a fool of myself in front of the whole class. But at the same moment, Mrs. White's decided to make her move from English teacher to stand-up comedian.

Shelby took a spot behind the podium. She looked out at the class. Angie was right. Half of them weren't even paying attention. Still, fifteen of them were. She noticed that Christie had pulled out a book of poetry. She was going to follow along in the book. If Shelby made the slightest mistake, Christie was ready to thrust her hand in the air and point it out. Vince and Angie each gave her encouraging looks.

Shelby took a deep breath. Then she remembered one thing that Vince had told her. She imagined that everyone in the room was a sack of potatoes. "You wouldn't be scared of French fries, would you?" he asked with that typical Vince logic. And he was right.

Shelby began to recite the poem and she did beautifully.

> Whose woods these are I think I know.
> His house is in the village, though;
> He will not see me stopping here
> To watch his woods fill up with snow.

Shelby could tell she was doing well because Christie looked frustrated. Mrs. White had a big smile on her face. Angie and Vince beamed like proud parents. This public speaking wasn't so bad after all. Shelby continued.

> My little horse must think it queer
> To stop without a farmhouse near
> Between the woods and frozen lake
> The darkest evening of the year.

Then Shelby stopped. Something about the poem was distracting her. Angie took a deep breath. Christie cracked a smile. Shelby tried to regain her composure. She couldn't remember the next line so she back-tracked to get her rhythm.

"Excuse me," Shelby said. "Let me go back a bit."

> To stop without a farmhouse near
> Between the woods and frozen lake

That's what was stumping her. "Frozen lake." Suddenly a big smile erupted on Shelby's face.

"I know who did it," she announced to the confused classroom.

"Duh," said Christie. "Robert Frost did it."

Mrs. White shot Christie a glare. Shelby looked at Angie and Vince.

"I know who did it," she said emphatically. They both smiled. She had solved the crime. Everything would have been great, except Shelby was still standing in front of all those people.

Even worse, because of her momentary lapse, now *everybody* was paying attention. And they didn't just look like fries anymore. They looked like curly-fries. Mean-spirited, evil, curly-fries.

Shelby took a deep breath and tried to resume where she had left off. She did it perfectly except for one thing—she spoke-sang it to the tune of Vince's song.

The class didn't know how to react. Even the teacher was at a loss. Then Angie stood up and gave her a standing ovation. Vince followed suit. Christie was perturbed.

"What are you so ga-ga about?" she asked them as she headed back toward her seat.

"Don't you get it," Angie started freewheeling. "What a brilliant statement about the poetic influences of popular culture." Now everyone was listening. And they were all confused—especially Shelby.

"I know who did it," Angie quoted, letting the words hang out there for everyone to consider. "She was pointing out that she, Shelby Woo, knew who really wrote the poem. Then she continued to show how to most other people the poem's just been trivialized into nothing more than a pop song." Angie shook her head in stunned amazement. "Brilliant, Shelby, brilliant."

"Encore," shouted Vince for no particular reason other than it seemed the thing to shout.

"Is that what you meant?" the teacher asked Shelby.

Shelby hadn't understood a word Angie said.

But she sure liked it better than the alternative. "Pretty much," Shelby concluded. "In a nutshell."

"Well, I am very impressed." Mrs. White started applauding. Pretty soon the entire class was into it. Except for Christie. The bell rang and they all streamed out of the door.

"You owe me big," Angie told her as the three of them went into the hall.

"I owe you both. I'll figure out a way to pay you back, but first I've got to call Detective Delancey. I think it's time she made an arrest."

Chapter
12

The executive board of the Sherlock Society was gathered in Everett Hood's private library. It was an imposing room—especially with the painting of the man who had founded the organization six decades earlier. It was precisely the sort of home-court advantage Hood wanted.

There were five members of the executive board. They included Everett Hood, Professor Lance Pickett, and the cockroach theorist who had legally changed his name from Melvin Jenkins to Sherlock Holmes.

"We are here to consider the dismissal of Mary

Longstreet as president of the Sherlock Society," Hood solemnly announced.

Just then there was a commotion at the door. It was Mary Longstreet and she was fighting her way past the butler. One of the board members had tipped her off to the meeting.

"Who do you think you are?" blasted Mary as she stormed into the room. "I was properly elected to serve as president of this organization."

"Yes," Hood hissed. "And you've done a dreadful job of it." His acid tone was not at all like the sweet one he had used with the kids.

"Just because I don't run it the way you would, doesn't mean . . ." They were interrupted by another commotion at the door.

"What now?" Hood said, barely able to control his anger. Again he went to the entryway, but this time he didn't recognize the face. It belonged to Sharon Delancey.

The detective flashed a warrant card and when the butler refused to move out of her way, she gave him a shoulder push she'd mastered during varsity field hockey.

Accompanying her was a detective from the Boston Police Department—the crime had occurred in both jurisdictions and they were working in tandem—as well as Shelby, Vince, and Angie.

"What may I ask is the meaning of this?" Hood bellowed.

"We're here to make an arrest in the theft of Allan Pinkerton's magnifying glass." Delancey always loved making that announcement. She let it sink in.

"You mean you've found it?" Professor Pickett asked.

"No," said Delancey. "But we know who took it." She let Shelby talk.

"The first thing we had to do," said Shelby, "was figure out who had a chance to steal it. Of all the people at the Mystery Ball, only three people had the opportunity—Mary Longstreet, Everett Hood, and Lance Pickett."

The three of them stared straight ahead.

"Then we had to figure out how the thief managed to get the magnifying glass out of the museum."

"It was the cockroaches, wasn't it?" said the Sherlock Holmes formerly known as Melvin Jenkins. "I knew it."

"No," said Detective Delancey. "I'm afraid it

wasn't the cockroaches." Holmes shot an angry glance at his Dr. Watson ventriloquist's dummy.

"It was the snow," announced Shelby. "The criminal dropped the magnifying glass from the terrace down into the snow covering the frozen lake." Professor Pickett took the opportunity to give himself an alibi.

"It couldn't have been me," he declared. "I never went out on the terrace."

"That may be true," said Delancey. "But there was a window right in the hall where you were sitting. You could have easily tossed it from there."

Pickett slunk back into his chair.

"Angie, Vince, and I found the spot where the magnifying glass fell. All we found there was dirt and something silver and shiny. We don't know what it is, though, because it fell to the bottom of the lake when the ice broke."

"This is leading somewhere, isn't it?" Mary implored.

Angie joined in with, "Then we made Shelby recite a poem in class."

"It was 'Stopping by Woods on a Snowy Evening,' " Vince interjected.

"That's when I realized you were guilty." Shelby was looking directly at Everett Hood.

"This is ridiculous," Hood cried. "What does Robert Frost have to do with anything? What happened to evidence and proof? Is this what the police force has become?"

"It was the line about the frozen lake in the poem," Shelby continued. "That's when I realized what was wrong with the crime scene. There was dirt mixed in with the snow."

"There's always dirt mixed with snow," Hood exclaimed.

"Not in a lake," said Shelby. "In a lake there should only be snow and ice. The dirt came from the plant."

"What plant," asked Holmes. Or was it the dummy?

"Mr. Hood buried the magnifying glass in a plant to help cushion its fall," Angie chimed in. "Then he threw both the plant and glass over the edge."

"That was the dead plant you had me throw away," Vince added.

"We sent two officers out to the lake today," Delancey said. "They were able to collect a pretty sizable amount of dirt. They're testing it right now to see if it matches the special dirt you have imported from Costa Rica."

"Bravo," Hood said mockingly. He sarcastically tapped the tip of his cane against the tile as if he were clapping.

"What happened to your cane?" asked Shelby.

"I don't know what you mean," he replied. "Although I'm sure you'll have some outlandish suggestion."

At the Mystery Ball, your cane had a silver tip.

"I blame all of this on you," he barked at Mary. "This event was poorly conceived from beginning to end. It will destroy the reputation of this organization." To emphasize his point, he rapped the floor with the silver tip of his cane.

But now the tip is missing.

"What happened to the silver tip from your cane?" Shelby asked Hood.

"It must have fallen off," he said. "I'm sure it's around here somewhere."

"No," Shelby said. "I'm sure it's at the bottom of the lake."

Hood was beaten. He looked up at the portrait of his grandfather, but he could offer no support. Delancey started to read him his rights and the detective from the Boston Police Department pulled out his handcuffs.

Everett Hood finally confessed and led the police to Allan Pinkerton's magnifying glass. It was buried in the pot of a Pink Revelation in his greenhouse.

He couldn't get over the fact that Mary had wanted to change the Sherlock Society so much. He wanted it to stay the way it was when his grandfather founded it. I guess we all need to be more open to change.

It turns out the seemingly bizarre behavior of Professor Pickett and Mary Longstreet was related. The professor did sell some Pinkerton artifacts, but they were ones he collected when he was doing his research. He sold them for fifty thousand dollars, which he then invested in *Eureka!* magazine. It was the same fifty thousand dollars Mary deposited in the bank. Pickett had read the brochure at the Mystery Ball while he was waiting in the hall and decided it would make an excellent magazine. Their first issue is going to have an article about how we solved the case. It'll be pretty neat, with glossy pictures and everything.

Vince also did something really sweet. He had all of our names engraved on his Detective of the Year trophy, since we solved it together. I like it. But not as much as I like the rose he gave me.

This place might turn out to be all right after all.

STOPPING BY WOODS
ON A SNOWY EVENING

by Robert Frost

Whose woods these are I think I know.
His house is in the village, though;
He will not see me stopping here
To watch his woods fill up with snow.

My little horse must think it queer
To stop without a farmhouse near
Between the woods and frozen lake
The darkest evening of the year.

He gives his harness bells a shake
To ask if there is some mistake.
The only other sound's the sweep
Of easy wind and downy flake.

The woods are lovely, dark, and deep,
But I have promises to keep,
And miles to go before I sleep,
And miles to go before I sleep.

About the Author

James Ponti started writing as a kid growing up in Atlantic Beach, Florida. He has written for newspapers, magazines, television shows, and movies. Among kids he's best known for writing at Nickelodeon, The Disney Channel and Sports Illustrated for Kids. He has been a writer for the television series of *The Mystery Files of Shelby Woo* since its first season. (His favorite episode is the one with the hurricane, called "Eye of the Storm.") He lives in Winter Park, Florida, with his wife, Denise, sons Alex and Grayson, and dog Lady. This is his first book of fiction.

Read Books. Earn Points. Get Stuff!

NICKELODEON® and
MINSTREL® BOOKS

Now, when you buy any book with the special Minstrel® Books/Nickelodeon "Read Books, Earn Points, Get Stuff!" offer, you will earn points redeemable toward great stuff from Nickelodeon!

Each book includes a coupon in the back that's worth points. Simply complete the necessary number of coupons for the merchandise you want and mail them in. It's that easy!

Nickelodeon Magazine.	4 points
Twisted Erasers	4 points
Pea Brainer Pencil	6 points
SlimeWriter Ball Point Pen	8 points
Zzand	10 points
Nick Embroidered Dog Hat	30 points
Nickelodeon T-shirt	30 points
Nick Splat Memo Board	40 points

- Each book is worth points (see individual book for point value)
- Minimum 40 points to redeem for merchandise
- Choose anything from the list above to total at least 40 points. Collect as many points as you like, get as much stuff as you like.

What? You want more?!?!
Then Start Over!!!

NICKELODEON/MINSTREL BOOKS POINTS PROGRAM

Official Rules

1. *HOW TO COLLECT POINTS*

Points may be collected by purchasing any book with the special Minstrel®/Nickelodeon "Read Books, Earn Points, Get Stuff!" offer. Only books that bear the burst "Read Books, Earn Points, Get Stuff!" are eligible for the program. Points can be redeemed for merchandise by completing the coupons (found in the back of the books) and mailing with a check or money order in the exact amount to cover postage and handling to Minstrel Books/Nickelodeon Points Program, P.O. Box 7777-G140, Mt. Prospect, IL 60056-7777. Each coupon is worth points. (See individual book for point value.) Copies of coupons are not valid. Simon & Schuster is not responsible for lost, late, illegible, incomplete, stolen, postage-due, or misdirected mail.

2. *40 POINT MINIMUM*

Each redemption request must contain a minimum of 40 points in order to redeem for merchandise.

3. *ELIGIBILITY*

Open to legal residents of the United States (excluding Puerto Rico) and Canada (excluding Quebec) only. Void where taxed, licensed, restricted, or prohibited by law. Redemption requests from groups, clubs, or organizations will not be honored.

4. *DELIVERY*

Allow 6-8 weeks for delivery of merchandise.

5. *MERCHANDISE*

All merchandise is subject to availability and may be replaced with an item of merchandise of equal or greater value at the sole discretion of Simon & Schuster.

6. *ORDER DEADLINE*

All redemption requests must be received by January 31, 1999, or while supplies last. Offer may not be combined with any other promotional offer from Simon & Schuster. Employees and the immediate family members of such employees of Simon & Schuster, its parent company, subsidiaries, divisions and related companies and their respective agencies and agents are ineligible to participate.

COMPLETE THE COUPON AND MAIL TO
NICKELODEON/MINSTREL POINTS PROGRAM
P.O. BOX 7777-G140
MT. PROSPECT, IL 60056-7777

NICKELODEON

MINSTREL® BOOKS

NAME_____

ADDRESS_____

CITY _____ STATE _____ ZIP _____

THIS COUPON WORTH FIVE POINTS
Offer expires January 31, 1999

I have enclosed _____ coupons and a check/money order (in U.S. currency only) made payable to "Nickelodeon/Minstrel Books Points Program" to cover postage and handling.

❏ 40–75 points (+ $3.50 postage and handling)

❏ 80 points or more (+ $5.50 postage and handling)

1464-01(2of2)